Storm Boy
and
Other Stories

Colin Thiele (pronounced Tee-lee) has published almost a hundred books during a writing career that spans more than fifty years. He was born in Eugunga, South Australia, and spent his childhood on a farm in the nearby ranges. He was schooled in the area, then went to the University of Adelaide where he was an outstanding successful student.

After service in the RAAF during the Second World War he became a high school and college lecturer, and eventually a principal and director. In 1945 he married Rhonda Gill, a teacher and artist, and they had two daughters – Janne and Sandy.

It was in 1958, during a seas voyage to the United States to take up a Fullbright Scholarship, that Colin Thiele wrote the first of his children's books. Since then he has become one of the best known and loved of Australian authors, and has received many awards and commendations for his work. In 1977 he was awarded the high honour of Companion of the Order of Australia (AC) for services to literature and education.

Feature films and television programs based on his books (*Storm boy, Blue Fin, The Fire in the Stone, The Water Trolley, and now Sun on the Stubble*) have been seen and acclaimed in main countries, and his work has been published extensively overseas – in China, Japan, Russia, South Africa and North America, England, and ten European countries.

In 1993 Colin and Rhonda Thiele moved to Dayboro, a small town north of Brisbane, Colin passed away in 2006.

COLIN THIELE

Storm Boy
and
Other Stories

NEW
HOLLAND

Published in Australia by
New Holland Publishers (Australia) Pty Ltd
Sydney • Auckland • London • Cape Town

www.newholland.com.au

1/66 Gibbes Street Chatswood NSW 2067 Australia2
18 Lake Road Northcote Auckland New Zealand
86 Edgware Road London W2 2EA United Kingdom
80 McKenzie Street Cape Town 8001 South Africa

First published as The Rim of the Morning 1966
Reprinted 1968, 1969, 1970, 1972
Seal Books edition 1974Reprinted 1976, 1978, 1980 (twice), 1981
Limp edition 1981
Film edition 1984
First published as Storm Boy and Other Stories
Paperback edition 1986
Reprinted 1988R
eprinted by Weldon Publishing 1990, 1991, 1992, 1993
Reprinted by Lansdowne Publishing Pty Ltd 1995, 1996, 1998 (twice), 1999
Reprinted by New Holland Publishers (Australia) Pty Ltd 2001, 2008, 2010, 2011

30

National Library of Australia Cataloguing-in-Publication Data:Thiele,
Colin, 1920–2006
Storm boy and other stories.
ISBN 9781864367669.
Pelicans–Juvenile fiction. I. Title.
A823.3

Wholly designed and typeset in Australia
Printer: Toppan Leefung Printing Limited (China)
Cover design by Robert G. Taylor , 2008, 2010

Contents

The Water Trolley

THE flames from the explosion were broad and flat in the sunlight, like yellow fans. Paul saw them flare above the pump even before the roar reached his ears. He was in the homestead yard saddling his pony, Peter, when the engine blew up, bringing the whole of their lives tumbling down in sudden strange confusion. But it wasn't until he saw his father stagger out of the smoke with his hands to his face and his clothes on fire that he really knew what had happened.

For the next few minutes Paul acted by instinct. He snatched the saddle-cloth from Peter's back, flung open the stockyard gate, and raced down towards the pump. "Dad! Dad!" he yelled. He didn't know who had told him, or how he had learnt it, but he knew that he had to wrap the cloth around his father to smother the flames. And he knew that he had to do it quickly.

His father was reeling forwards, still clutching at his face with one hand and beating blindly and ineffectually at his clothing with the other. Paul dashed up to him and flung the cloth around his waist. Then he seized the charred shirt. It came away like rotten rag, what was left of it, and he desperately stripped off the bits of smouldering sleeve.

"Down, Dad!" he panted. "Roll on the ground."

But his father, dazed and blinded with shock, didn't seem to understand. And so Paul smothered the fire with his saddle-rug and tore away the ashy pieces of cloth until there were only tatters left. From the beginning he could see that his father was badly hurt. He had been sprayed with petrol from the exploding engine, and his face and eyes had been seared by the blast. His hair was almost completely burnt away. He clutched heavily at Paul's shoulder. "The house," he gasped. "Must get . . . up to the house." Paul was already struggling to obey. Half leading, half supporting him, he stumbled erratically towards the house, terribly aware of the agony of his father's burnt flesh beside him. Luckily Paul was strong. Although only twelve years old, he had the shoulders and muscles of a lad of fifteen.

Behind them, ironic and mocking, he could hear the cool sound of running water. He glanced back and saw what had happened. The force of the explosion from the pumping plant had hurled bits of metal about like shrapnel, and some of them had gone up through the bottom of the big storage tank that supplied the homestead with water. He felt a desperate sense of urgency and alarm. As soon as his father had been attended to he must hurry back and try to plug the leaks. Water was priceless, especially just now in the middle of summer with the big dam dry and the worst of the heat still to come. In fact, it was just this emergency that had led to the accident; his father had gone down that morning to get the pump on the homestead bore working again, and while he was there something had happened—a spark perhaps, a backfire, a moment of carelessness with the drum of petrol. Whatever the cause, there was now neither pump nor water.

Paul's mother came hurrying out on to the veranda and stared down at them in fear and unbelief.

"Mum!" Paul called. "Quick, Mum! Dad's been hurt!"

She ran down to meet them. "Harold!" Her voice trembled for a second, and Paul could see the look of terror in her eyes. But he was glad she didn't cry out or make a fuss. Instead, she quickly took some of the weight on herself and together they got his father inside. There they took off his boots and stripped away the rest of the charred cloth before getting him into bed. Paul could see her hands trembling as she worked.

"Wait here!" she said a little breathlessly, and ran out, leaving Paul to watch at his father's bedside. A minute later he could hear her voice at the transceiver, calling up the Flying Doctor.

"Able Baker Zeke calling V.J.D. Able Baker Zeke calling V.J.D. Medical! Emergency!" And soon the reply was coming in loud and clear. All the morning's radio gossip was whipped from the air in an instant—the exchange of recipes, the tales of children's illnesses—and the whole Inland knew that there'd been an accident on Munlacowie Station. The engine at the pumping plant had exploded and the boss was badly hurt.

"Keep him warm," the reassuring voice of the doctor was saying, "and give him a sedative if you can. Have you got anything? Over."

"Only aspirin, doctor. And maybe some Veganin or something. Will they do? Over."

"Fine, Mrs Anderson. Is he fully conscious?"

"No, doctor, only semi-conscious. The explosion, you see, as well as the burns. . . . Over."

Paul heard the catch in his mother's voice and knew how hard she was fighting to keep going.

3

"We'll leave right away, Mrs Anderson. There'll be a hospital bed waiting for him here as soon as we get back. Over."

"Thank you, doctor. When do you expect to pick him up? Over."

"As soon as we can. Before noon. Over."

"Thank you. Do hurry, won't you? Over."

"We will. And remember to keep him still and warm, Mrs Anderson. Over."

"Yes, doctor. Thank you. Over."

"Over and out."

It was a long wait for the Flying Doctor. After Paul and his mother had given his father the sedative, they sat by the bedside, waiting and listening. It was only when Paul's two little sisters, Mary and Helen, came clattering in from their game in the laundry that the anxious silence was broken.

"Take them outside," Paul's mother said. "Try to keep them away from the house."

Paul did his best to entertain them, but it was nearly an hour before he heard the familiar drone of the plane as it swept in over the house and landed on the strip near by.

After that things moved so quickly there was no time to think. Mr Anderson was carried out on a stretcher, there were a few hasty goodbyes, and before they quite knew what had happened the plane had taken off again and was dwindling away into the empty sky.

As they watched the speck waver and disappear a great loneliness seemed to crowd in on them. "When Daddy coming back in a . . . in a airplane?" Helen asked. She was hardly three, and had no real idea of what had happened. But Mary was seven, and had

4

to be kept from pestering them with tearful questions. Paul could see that his mother was closer to breaking down than she wanted to admit, so he took his sisters and handed them over to Lily and Lena, the two aboriginal helpers in the kitchen. Then, when his mother had gone inside to rest, he slipped out into the baking sunlight again.

It was only then that he suddenly remembered something. Something urgent. Nobody had sealed the holes in the water tank.

CHAPTER ONE

THE tank was empty. Huge and hollow as a drum it stood, the five thousand gallons from its big-bellied paunch all drained away. Usually the rows of heavy posts under the tank looked like Atlases with bent shoulders, supporting the world on their backs, but now they seemed to be jokingly balancing a bloated ping-pong ball on their fingertips.

Paul climbed the ladder to the top and peered in through the manhole. It was dim and damp inside, and the rank smell of decay rose up in his face like steam. He could see the holes clearly—three, four, five ragged patches of light in the dark sludge. It would take real men to repair damage like that: men with rivets and galvanized iron patching plates. Plasterers even. The whole thing might have to be cemented out.

He stood on the topmost rung of the ladder, balancing on the balls of his feet . . . thinking. He could

5

see far out across the station. Under the wide brim of his hat his eyes were puckered. The glare leapt up from the plains, and the ridges to the north ran molten and sluggish with heat. Munlacowie! The Meeting Place of Water! Not any more. Even the creek that had given the aborigines their meeting place was a dry meander now, picked out by a straggle of old coolibahs and gums that refused to die. How deep they must be driving their roots, forcing them down like fierce fingers fighting for life, through the sand and rock to the shrinking moisture below.

It was water from under the ground that would have to supply them now. The whole station—cattle, sheep, horses, trees, poultry, people. Most of the men were continually out at the bores these days, cleaning the troughs, checking the pumps and windmills, bringing in weakening stock. All except Harry Boyle and Billy the Dill who had driven the truck down to the railhead to pick up some spare parts a couple of days before, and two or three of the boundary-riders who were still down south on holiday. And so the homestead was almost deserted. Mrs Boyle was over at Kulkaroo, a hundred miles to the east, visiting her sister, and Miss Hastings, the governess, was still down in Adelaide. She'd be back in a week or so, when the schools reopened again after the Christmas holidays.

Paul climbed down from the tank and pressed his footprints into the damp sand under the tank-stand. Already the heat of midday was drying the surface, and the edges were crumbling and running together. It was frightening. Five thousand gallons soaked up in an hour, swallowed without a trace. No wonder the dams and creeks were dry.

An impatient whinny roused him and he stopped

short with a shock. It was Peter! He was still hitched to the stockyard rails, half saddled and bridled, just as he'd been left that morning at the moment of the explosion. Paul ran to him.

"Peter! Peter! You poor old fellow." He started to strip off the saddle. "Been standing here all the morning in the heat." The pony flicked his ears in annoyance. "About time too," his gaze said. "What a way to treat your friends."

They were friends, of course. Inseparable. That was how Peter had got his name. When, after years of pestering, Paul had finally been given his pony, he couldn't be parted from it. Mrs Anderson had even threatened to sell it because Paul insisted on taking it into his room with him and had once frightened the wits out of poor little Mary when she had toddled in unexpectedly and come face to face with a monster. But Paul's father had only laughed. "Sorry, Paul," he'd said, "but you'll have to part with Peter at night."

"Peter?" asked Mrs Anderson, puzzled.

"Well, they're inseparable, aren't they? Where Paul goes, there Peter goes too."

The name stuck. From then on the boy and his horse were Paul and Peter.

But today Peter seemed angry even after he'd been set free. He tossed his head and walked stiffly down to the water trough. Paul walked beside him, patting the pony's fine smooth throat and rubbing the velvet of his nose.

"Sorry, boy," he said. "It was all because of the accident." Peter slurped from the bottom of the trough and Paul watched the long ripple of his swallow move along his throat. The water level was very low, and the air sucked noisily round his nostrils. Then Paul

7

saw the ball-cock. Its arm hung down uselessly and the ball rested on the bottom of the trough like an Eastern priest pressing his forehead to the ground. In that position, the tap was wide open and the water should have been streaming into the trough. Paul felt a pang of fear. There wasn't any water!

For the first time he saw clearly what the accident had done. Apart from the injuries to his father, it had suddenly placed the whole homestead in danger. There wasn't a drop of surface water within five miles, and there were no men except old Moses left to get the pumping plant going again. Moses was an ancient rouseabout, over eighty years old, half deaf, and as gnarled as a rock-rooted myall. He wouldn't be able to help. Yet it was only Tuesday now, and it wasn't likely that any of the other men would come in before the end of the week. Even Harry Boyle and Billy the Dill couldn't be expected back in the truck before Thursday, especially if they met some of their mates in the pub down at the railway siding.

That left two or three days at least, perhaps four or five, before they could expect any help. And even after some of the men had come back it would probably take them a day or two to get the plant working again. What, Paul wondered, would the homestead do in the meantime? There was still a rung of fresh water in one of the house tanks, but that was strictly for drinking and cooking. In the meantime there were four horses in the yard besides Peter, two cows, a calf, a hundred or more fowls, and the daily demands of station life for washing, scrubbing, and cleaning. He could drive the horses out to one of the bores on the run and just leave them to fend for themselves, but he couldn't very well do that with the cows and fowls.

8

He smiled at the thought of droving a hundred white leghorn pullets and roosters across the saltbush plain. But the smile didn't last long. It was too hot and menacing for that. Somehow they would have to get water, if only a few gallons, to tide them over.

Paul walked over to the bore, scuffing the dust. The signs of the morning's disaster were still clear enough; the whole engine had been torn from its mountings, and bits of debris lay scattered everywhere. The shaft and the connecting rods to the pump seemed to be undamaged, but there was no power to drive them. He gazed about hopelessly. Even if another engine, from the shearing sheds, say, could be improvised for the job, he would never have the strength to bring it over and connect it up. And engines could be dangerous too; one had almost killed his father. Perhaps it would have been better if people had stuck to windmills.

Windmills! Paul felt a quick twinge of excitement. The huge tower of the old windmill that had once done all the station pumping still rose above him, the metal fans of the wheel held motionless like an unchanging daisy against the sky. Only during the last few years had its work been taken over by the clacking engine that fussed and fumed and smelt of sludgy oil, but as far as Paul knew, the great old mill was still in good order.

Of course it hadn't been allowed to work; the brake-lever was lashed down hard, and the tail and the big wheel were locked together by a steel chain, so that no matter what kind of gale blew up, the fans could never turn. They could only butt and clank and swivel in the wind like a crazy weathercock. Then, to render it completely powerless, a six-foot section of the

9

plunger-shaft had been uncoupled so that, even if the fans did escape some day and start whirling again, the piston would just bob up and down uselessly, prodding the empty air.

But none of these things daunted Paul. He knew where the disconnected shaft was kept in the harness shed, and ran to get it. The pins were rusted, but he was able to loosen them at last with a few dabs of kerosene. Then he carried the shaft back to the windmill, climbed a few feet up the rungs and, after a minute of jockeying and pushing, slipped the bolts back into place. The plunger-arm was complete again, and the mill was ready to come back to life. But first he had to unchain it and set it free.

He loosened the rusty wire that bound the brake and released the lever. Then he started to climb the tower. And now, for the first time, he was afraid. He had never had much to do with heights before, and when he looked back he was astonished to see how far the ground had receded and how small the posts and fences were. Even the homestead itself had become a toy model on a map—the buildings arranged in blocks, the stables, sheds, and drafting yards no bigger than the parts of a Meccano set, and the horses like Noah's Ark animals fixed to the ground they stood on.

He quickly turned his gaze upwards again and went on climbing. The windmill had grown huge. He had never realized how big it was until now. He could have stood upright in the inner wheel and still had the blades of the fans stretching two or three feet beyond him. It had a disconcerting habit, too, of swinging about from side to side, so that no matter from which direction Paul tried to approach the platform behind it, the wheel suddenly swung round like an iron shutter and cut him off. He was surprised, too, at the movement of air. Whereas it had seemed a hot, still afternoon down in the station yard, up here on top of the tower there was quite a breeze. It wasn't a wind so much as a series of petulant little swirls that set the wheel groaning in its chains and made the tail buck angrily. To Paul there was a sense of malice about it, resentment at being chained up for two years when all the time the free winds had raced and sung through the steel lattice-work like rigging, and pressed on the broad palms of the fans.

He gained the platform at last and crouched there, clinging to the tapering steel uprights and ducking to avoid the tail whenever it threatened to brush him off like a fly. Then, as he got his breath back, he carefully started to unwind the chain. He soon realized what a dangerous and difficult job it was. The tail had been lashed back until its broad vane was almost parallel to the wheel, instead of streaming out at right angles behind it. The pressure from the tail, straining to spring back into position, was strong and constant, and it was only by using all his strength and waiting for the lulls between gusts, that Paul was at last able to unhitch the chain and free the wheel.

What happened next he never clearly remembered. There was a puff of wind, the blades suddenly spun in front of his eyes, and the plunger started pistoning up and down. The next instant the whole tower vibrated, there was the grinding sound of tearing metal, and the main pumping shaft shattered beneath him. He looked down quickly, forgot about the tail, and was struck a swinging blow on the neck. He lost his balance, clutched frantically for a handhold, and for a terrible second actually dangled from the tail-frame sixty feet above the ground like a struggling grub. Miraculously he was able to get his feet on the landing again and heave himself back.

For a long time Paul just crouched there, clinging to the tower. The huge wheel spun in front of his eyes, and the tail swung above his head. They were like two living things playing a deadly game of cat and mouse with him. But at last, when there was a lull for a second or two, he swung himself on to the steel rungs of the ladder and climbed down breathlessly. When he reached the ground his hands shook and the muscles in his arms jerked with exhaustion. He went over to the brake and pulled the lever down hard. Above him he saw the tail swing in and the wheel slowly stop.

"That'll have to hold you," he said fiercely. "The chain can wait. I wouldn't go up there again today to let you have another go at me. Not for a million pounds."

He stood gazing up through the centre of the tower, its lacework of steel tapering high above him like a spider's funnel. Part of the plunger-rod still hung down the centre, bent and broken like a piece of torn web. He wondered what had gone wrong. A rusted joint perhaps, a weak connection, a faulty realignment of lengths and angles on the pumping shaft when it had been replaced. Whatever it was, it had smashed the rod to pieces. There'd be no more pumping of water by that old mill.

Paul hung his head and kicked at the dust as he always did when he was sad and angry and beaten. Why didn't they have a full-scale artesian bore on Munla-cowie, like some of the other stations? A bore that spouted water above the ground, millions of gallons of it, rushing up so fast and so far that it came out boiling hot and raced off steaming and sparkling into dams and storage tanks. No pumps needed, no engines, no windmills. Just a man-made hole in the ground a mile deep. He scuffed at the dust again. But not on Munlacowie. Here there wasn't a single well like that. There was plenty of underground water, of course, and his father had put down more than a dozen bores. But they were all sub-artesian; the water had to be pumped. It didn't ever quite rise to the surface, and so had to be helped up the last few stages, given a lift out, so to speak. And when the lift broke down, as it had now, the water just didn't arrive.

He went up through the houseyard gate, past a couple of empty forty-gallon drums, and hung up his hat under the veranda. Instinctively he went to the hand basin in the corner and turned on the tap. There was no water. It came as a physical shock to him. Even though he had been the first to know what had happened, he still had to keep on rediscovering it. He looked at his hands, grimy from the rust and grease of the windmill. What was the use of soap, if there was nothing to wet it with.

The more Paul moved about, the more he saw that the simplest everyday things depended on water, and the more impossible he knew it would be to exist without it. They must have water—just a bit, to tide them over until the men came back. A drum or two would do it. His heart gave a little flip. A drum or two! Like the ones by the gate. He could *cart* it from the nearest bore on the run. Though the truck and Land-Rover were both away on other jobs he could use the old trolley by the shearing shed. Peter could pull it all right, and the tray was big enough to hold a couple of drums with comfort. Eighty gallons. That would see them through easily.

As soon as he had made up his mind Paul went inside. His mother was up, but he could see that she'd been crying. He had never experienced anything like this before, and it made him uncomfortable, so he avoided looking at her and concentrated on the important question.

"Mum," he said, "I've got to go out to the Gidgee Bore first thing tomorrow morning and get a load of water."

His mother looked up sharply. "Don't be silly, Paul. Whatever gave you that idea?"

"Because there's none left in the big tank, and the horses and cows and fowls need it. 'Specially in this heat."

"None left in the big tank! What do you mean?"

"The explosion blew holes in it and the water ran out. There's none left. Not a drop!"

"What about the bore?"

"There's no pump. The engine's messed up and the windmill won't work." Paul stopped, waiting for the news to sink in. "And there's no one here to fix them."

"But how could you cart it?"

"In forty-gallon drums."

"How?"

"On the old horse-trolley. Peter can pull it like a toy."

His mother was uneasy. The shock of the accident, and now this sudden new danger, had filled her with fear. She was afraid to let Paul go.

"But the Gidgee Bore is such a long way, Paul . . . and the track is so rough."

"It's only five miles. I could do it in a couple of hours."

"With a full water tank?"

"With a couple of drums. Even if we couldn't do better than a mile an hour, I'd still be back before lunch."

"And what good would it do?"

"It'd save the stock—the calves and poultry and that."

"For a couple of days!"

"Till the men get back. Gosh, Mum, even *we* couldn't last without water. Up here in the house I mean."

"And what if . . . if I have to fly down to the hospital; if your father is so badly hurt?"

"We could still look after the place . . . 'slong as we had the water; old Moses and me, and Lily and Lena."

His mother sighed, and picked at the seam of her dress with her fingers. Paul knew the sign. He had seen her do it so often when she was about to surrender under protest.

"All right then, Paul, if you must. But promise that you won't be long."

"I'll be back before lunch-time tomorrow. I'll get everything ready this arvo and make a start before daylight."

He got up and smiled self-consciously at her as he went out. "And don't worry, Mum. It'll just be a pleasant little run."

But before long those words tasted like ashes in his mouth.

CHAPTER TWO

PAUL set off at half past four. He had spent most of the previous afternoon getting things ready. The old trolley was a crazy thing with iron tyres, cracked shafts, and a loose tray; it had taken him two hours to get a bit of grease on to the axles and wheel-boxes, and to brace the shafts and nail down all the loose cross-pieces. Then he'd had to roll the two drums on board, stand them upright, and lock them in position with three or four heavy wooden chocks.

"Crude but sturdy." It was the phrase his father often used, and Paul could hear it in his imagination now as he looked at his handiwork. He smiled. But it would do the job and that was all that mattered.

Peter's opinion of the trolley was poorer than Paul's. He snorted in disgust when he saw it, and backed away. If it hadn't been for the experience he'd had with shafts and carts when pulling the children's jinker round the yard, Paul would never have got him into the harness at all. As it was, he pretended to shy at the collar and hames, and pranced back on the chains when Paul was coupling them up.

At last everything was ready. Paul sat on the front of the trolley with his legs dangling and flicked the reins. Peter minced and danced for a second or two, but then he pulled forward strongly, the trolley lurched off, and Paul—after swaying back so suddenly that only the reins saved him from being flung on his back with his feet in the air—settled down to the clatter and bump of the trip.

The world around him was easing itself gently into that strange half light between darkness and dawn. The moon was fading, but a hint of silver still lay like dew over the roofs and ridges. The trees along Munlacowie Creek stood out clearly—a meandering line of black mushrooms rooted in shadow. A mile or two beyond them rose the blunt square tops of the Tables, a cluster of tent hills or mesas, butting gloomily at the skyline in the half light. They were really the last remnants of a vast ancient plain that had once covered most of Central Australia, broken down and eroded over thousands of years into these stony monuments like flat-topped pyramids.

Beyond them, Paul knew, were two sandy dunes that the station men called the Big Ridge and the Little Ridge, then another dry creek bed, the Washaway, and at last the wide endless sameness of the Gidgicowie Plain. And the Gidgee Bore was right on the edge of the plain, less than a hundred yards from the creek.

Paul swung his legs as the trolley jolted along. The total distance from the homestead to the bore was five miles, perhaps a little under, so he knew he could reach it by six o'clock. Allowing an hour to fill the two drums, though he was certain he could do it in twenty minutes, he would be ready to return by seven. And even if he averaged no more than a mile an hour on the way back he would still be home before lunch, just as he had told his mother.

Peter stepped out perkily. They trundled down the track to the Munlacowie Creek, gathered speed down the bank, and then plunged suddenly into silence and slowness when the wheels hit the sand in the creekbed and the iron tyres sank in. But Peter pulled hard, thudding his forefeet down and straining at the load so that presently they emerged between the trees on the far side and struck northwards towards the gap in the Tables.

And now the darkness was draining away and the east was awash with light. The edges and angles of the hills ahead stood out clearly as they drove towards them. At the entrance to the gap where the track led between two big table tops Paul stopped to give Peter a rest. He guessed that it must be near five o'clock. The sky was an ever-changing pearl shell as the tides of light came sweeping in with the dawn.

Colour bloomed across the east—dove grey at first, with touches of blue and yellow, growing quickly to saffron and orange, and finally bursting into spears of pink and red. The line of the horizon shimmered and hardened. The sky looked shining and metallic, like a brass gong waiting to be struck. Paul waited. He never failed to feel the surge of the desert sunrise, its beauty and power and terror, as if the sun were leaping up afresh to finish the work of yesterday—not the warm-hearted entry of a Greek god, but a fierce desert gurra wielding his whips of fire.

Now the sky rang with light like a million trumpets. There! No, not quite yet! The horizon quivered in the glow. Now! A sudden shaft shot out at his face, as the great globe of the sun thrust up its burning disc and slowly rose clear of the land.

Paul turned. "Come on, Peter! Sun's up!" And the trolley trundled off into the gap between the hills.

There were gibbers and hard flinty bits of scree strewn about the track here, and the two empty water-drums boomed and rumbled. Paul found the ride too rough, so he jumped off and walked beside the trolley, holding the reins like an ancient ploughman as the iron wheels plunged and jerked along. Whenever there was

18

a bigger jolt than usual the drums clanged together more violently and the echoes went tolling and reverberating across the morning like the rumbling of the Rainbow Serpent who, according to the legends of the aborigines, lived deep in the caves of the earth and unwound his coils like thunder.

Shadows as big as mountains stretched away in front of him. As they passed close beside the biggest of the tent hills, the one the men called Old Table Top, Paul could see the sharp dividing line between sunshine and shadow. It was almost like looking at an eclipse. On the eastern side the edges of the hard crust that formed the table top stood out clearly in the sun. The light slanted against it in enormous parallel rays like long-handled brushes touching the crest with gold till it glowed. The hard rock ended in a cliff as steep as a wall—the "breakaway," people called it—but under it the softer layers had been gouged and scoured by the wind until in places there were hollows and niches that looked like dragons' caves. Paul had often fossicked about in them, especially on the southern side where the walls and rocks were covered by strange aboriginal carvings and paintings in ochre—outlines of human hands that glowed white in the gloom, and strange totem signs and creatures like prehistoric kangaroos and wombats as big as bears. Below the caves the hill sloped away in tumbled masses of broken stone and bushy knolls covered with tussocks of porcupine grass.

Sometimes in the evenings the tent hills were sombre places, breathing the spirit of the ancient tribes of the past and the strange power of their legends. But this morning there was none of that. The air was already warm and the light was as bright as brass.

"Giddee-up!" Paul called above the rattle of the

trolley, and, shaping his lips very carefully and deliberately, he started to whistle *Waltzing Matilda* as vigorously as he could. When they emerged from the line of flat-topped hills they passed into a belt of open country with a scattering of saltbush and tussock, until they came to the Big Ridge—the first of the two old sand dunes that ran across their track like long embankments. Although it was what the geologists called a consolidated dune, where the sand had stopped drifting and bits of rooty vegetation had fixed the grains and bound the ridge together, the track was still loose and crumbly enough to make walking hard. Poor little Peter puffed and panted so much that when they eventually got to the top Paul called a long halt.

It was the highest part of the track. Beyond the second ridge he could see the far disc of the plain—a vast sweep that stretched on and on until it met the firm clean curve of the horizon. Paul puckered his eyes and tried to penetrate the distance. He imagined he could see the huge salt lakes of the inland—a crescent of salt as flat as a skating rink, and as harsh to life as the land of Lot's wife. But all he could really see was a corner of the Gidgicowie Plain, no more than a pocket handkerchief in a land where he could have walked on for a thousand miles trapped like a fly beneath the moving bowl of the sky.

Paul knew the vastness and emptiness of the land around him. He could feel it in his bones. And in a strange way he loved it. In the twelve years of his life he had seen enough of the heat and drought, of dust and death, and of two summer floods when the Munlacowie Creek was a river three miles wide, to know that the Inland didn't deal in half measures. But he liked it that way. Sunlight sharper than knives, shadows as firm as posts, heat that struck through to his marrow. And colour! Harsh golden fanfares in the morning, quivering hazes of blue at midday when the distances danced as filmy and fine as gossamer; and in the evening, when the west had grown over the sun, the world burnt red and black, and fumes rose out of the desert, smoking and smouldering along the horizon like sullen bushfires.

But this was no time for dreaming. The day was awake and the bore was still more than a mile away.

"Come on, Peter!" he called. "Wakey! Wakey!" And they trundled off down the slope, the wheels silent in the sand and the drums booming together softly every now and then like muffled didgeridoos. A few hundred yards further on they came to the second dune—the Little Ridge—and panted their way to the top. It was only half the size of its big brother, but Paul's legs were slowing down in the sand and he was glad to stop for a short rest again.

The bore was dead ahead of them now, the windmill, tanks and troughs standing out boldly on the plain a short distance beyond the dry creekbed of the Washaway. There was a straggle of trees along the creek, scribbly coolibahs rooted in the broad, sandy basin of the channel. And between the creek and the Little Ridge where Paul stood lay half a mile of flat plain, dun-coloured and dry, with a scattering of porcupine grass and a few old dead roly-poly bushes. The silence of the morning and the great solitude of distance lay all round them. But again Paul knew he had to break it.

"Last lap ahead," he said. "Come on, boy." He flicked the reins and they bowled off down the gentle slope of the dune and out on to the plain.

And now, suddenly, they were intruders. As they approached the Washaway with trolley-boards rattling and water-drums booming they startled the emptiness into life. A flock of galahs took off from the creek, exploding out of the coolibahs in a flurry of wings and feathers, flashing pink and pearl-grey in the sunlight and setting the whole sky on edge with fierce shrieks. The sound was as harsh as metal, as grating to Paul's ear as fingernails on iron.

"Noisy galoots," he shouted. "Why don't you kick up a din?" For answer a group of stragglers shrieked up from the remaining trees and went off yelling after the others. There they smoothed themselves into the main flock, and the whole body, banking suddenly in a great blaze of pink, streamed away to the east.

The noise set the place in motion. As the trolley emerged from the Washaway two emus, unnoticed before in the shadow of the tank by the bore, went lolloping off across the plain, thrusting out their knobby knees and strong straight legs as thick as saplings, and rustling their tails like ridiculous dusters. Five euros, who had been drinking at the troughs, stood up as stiff as sticks, their ears frozen, nostrils lifted, and forepaws tensed in front of their chests. For a few seconds they were statues, heads all in line, eyes fixed in strange amazement at the juggernaut rumbling towards them. Then they, too, broke their formation and leapt away at angles in a burst of quick bounds and staccato hops until, swinging into a rhythm of long driving leaps, they dwindled towards the horizon still arching and bucking in the distance like enormous fleas.

As Paul and Peter trundled up to the troughs, a hawk rose lazily above them and hung in the air calmly and insolently. A goanna, surprised in the cool, damp shade under the tank, raised his head in fierce unbelief, threatened their intrusion for a second with his beady eyes, and then took off in the direction of the trees like a swift grey shadow, his feet a disembodied blur between the ground and the arrow of his body.

"Talk about visitors," said Paul to Peter. "You can hardly move for them." But Peter didn't hear. He had his mouth and nose in the water of the trough and was slurping noisily and thirstily.

"All right," Paid said. "So you're thirsty! But you could mind your manners. Now I know why we never give you soup." Peter tossed his head impatiently and went on drinking.

"*Hisssss!*" It was an angry sizzle right beside Paul's ear. He jumped in alarm. "Crikey," he said aloud. "A bloomin' old beardy." It was a frillneck, bristling and seething with annoyance. His frill stood out as big as an Elizabethan collar, his head framed in it like the centre of a weird black flower. His mouth was wide open, as purple as night, and his flat, scaly body was hard and iron-grey as if he'd crawled out of a foundry forge or a lava pit long ago when lizards were made out of fire and ashes. He was anchored on top of the big corner-post by the tank-stand—a sort of ancient gargoyle sent to guard the priceless gift of water.

"All right, beardy! No need to be so snooty about it," Paul said. "I'm just going to get a bit of water." He crawled up and checked the level in the tank. "Anyone'd think we'd sunk this bore for the likes of you. Go on, move over." He pushed at the frillneck with his boot, but the lizard swung round in an arc and faced him, his eyes blazing.

"Well, all right, if you're going to be difficult. But

23

see that you stay where you are. I'm not going to have you creeping about all over the place while I'm taking on the load. Next thing I s'pose it'll be snakes." And Paul, half fearful of his own suspicions, looked round carefully before preparing to fill the drums.

CHAPTER THREE

So far things had been going according to plan. The outward trip had taken rather longer than Paul had reckoned, chiefly because of their pauses for rest on the sandhills; but it was not yet seven o'clock and the rest of the job looked simple enough. Still, there was no point in dawdling. It was going to be hot, very hot. The daily temperatures had been rising for a week and they were obviously building up to a climax now. The breeze, which had been hopping about fitfully for days, was settling into a northerly, and its breath, as Paul's father would have said, was as dry as a lime-burner's boot. The sooner they got back home the better.

When Peter had finished drinking, Paul took him by the bit and led him forward until the trolley was near the tank-stand and the two drums stood directly beneath the stop-cock. This was really a huge tap set in a two-inch outlet pipe. It had to be opened with a big metal spanner that turned a brass cylinder inside the pipe until it reached a point where the two apertures coincided, allowing the water to rush out. Then, by hitching a short piece of old guttering to the outlet, the water-carter could guide the flow wherever he wanted it. Paul took the guttering, tied one end to the outlet, and rested the other on the rim of the first drum. Then he took the spanner from its hook under the tank-stand, fitted it over the square brass head of the tap, and pulled. It wouldn't budge.

He took a new grip, braced one foot firmly against the corner-post, and pulled with all his power. The tap held firm. Twice more he tried, but failed. He took the spanner and used it as a hammer, jarring the cylinder as hard as he could. It was caked with salty encrustations and mineral deposits from the hard bore water. Nobody had carted water from Gidgicowie for years, and everything was stiff with disuse. After five minutes' knocking and scraping Paul took the spanner and tried again. Still no movement. As a last desperate measure he stood up on the tank-stand, clung against the face of the tank like a tarantula, and pressed the sole of his boot on the spanner with all his strength. For a moment he thought it moved, but it was the spanner itself, not the tap. He took up a new position and tried again. Suddenly the square corners of the brass nut sheared off. Paul's foot shot away from under him, he came down heavily, and his ribs hit the pipe before he rolled off and fell six feet to the ground.

For a while he lay there numb with pain. Then he got up slowly, still holding his side, and limped round the trolley two or three times. Gingerly he pulled up his shirt. A long red weal ran down across his ribs from his left armpit, ending in a big bruise already turning blue-black like old ink. He pressed it gently. Although he winced, it seemed to be a surface pain, rather than any deep-seated injury. He swung his arm vigorously and took two or three deep breaths. There was no undue pain. He tucked in his shirt again and went back to the tank. At least no bones were broken, and apart from some soreness for a while he should be able to finish the job as if nothing had happened.

One thing was certain, though. The stop-cock and gravity gutter were useless now. He would have to fill both drums by hand, ladling the water up in buckets from the ball-tap by the trough. He brought the trolley round again and backed it up as close as he could. Then he took the battered old bore-bucket and started work.

It was a dreadful job—tedious and tiring. The water from the ball-tap was fed through a half-inch pipe, partly clogged and narrowed like an old artery, so that the flow into the bucket was a mere trickle. Paul had so much time between each bucketful that he soon found himself calculating how long it would be before he was finished. If the bucket held two gallons and each drum held forty, he would need twenty buckets-ful to the drum. And because it took at least two minutes to fill the bucket at the tap he would need forty minutes for each drum, perhaps longer. That meant an hour and a half altogether. At this rate it would be nine o'clock before he could start the return journey, and there was little likelihood that he would be home by noon as he had promised. And if he weren't, his mother would start to worry.

The heat was growing fierce now, and the breeze was freshening. There was a vindictive note in the way it strummed the bands of flat iron on the mill-tower and chanted a low note among the crevices of the tank-stand. Out on the plain it was starting to fling up little scurries of dust as if flicking the earth with hot whips. He remembered old Harry Boyle, who'd been a seaman years before, talking about the menace

26

of the rising wind: when the first white-caps start breaking on the sea, and the first dust-waves start pepperin' the Inland, why then it's time to batten down, Paul, boy. Time to start battening down.

Paul turned back to the bucket. The first drum was still barely half full though he seemed to have been at it for hours. There was another bucket under the tank—a battered, crumpled old thing pricked with pin-holes of light when Paul held it up to the sun. But even if he could have used it, the slow splatter from the tap couldn't be made to flow any faster. Unless he dipped from the trough! Of course! One of the drums, the one filled from the tap, could be set aside with clean water for use in the house; the other one, filled from the trough, could be used in the yard for the animals and fowls. He dipped the old bucket into the trough and swung it up in an arc to the second drum. It was an idea he should have thought of long before.

But with two buckets the strain was twice as great. He had to keep one eye continually on the flow of the tap as he ladled vigorously from the trough; then he had to run to the tap, heave the full bucket up to the lip of the clean drum, and start the whole process over again. His boots squelched and the tray of the trolley was awash with spilt water, but at least the drums were filling.

After half an hour Paul had slowed to a droop. The muscles of his arms felt like pieces of stretched elastic, and the bruise in his side throbbed with pain. He could no longer heave the buckets up to the drums from the ground. Instead, he stood them on the tray, clambered up after them, and then emptied each one in turn. But this was very tiring work, too. The constant lifting and climbing left him exhausted, and now he was glad of the delay caused by the slowness of the tap.

But at last the water began to lap the brims of both drums. Paul climbed down stiffly, offered Peter a last drink, and then threw both buckets under the tank-stand. "Boy," he said, panting and mopping his face, "I hope nobody has to do *that* again for a year or two. First thing I've got to get Dad to do is to fix that stop-cock. . . ." He bit his lip . . . Dad wouldn't be about the place to fix things this summer; at least, not for a long time, even if things went well. He wondered how his father was. On an operating table, perhaps, or fighting for his life in the clean white antiseptic world of the hospital at the Flying Doctor base. The thought was enough to rouse him. With Dad away, it was his job to be back at the station himself. You never knew what help Mum needed at a time like this. She might even have to go down to join Dad at the base.

Peter quivered his fetlock and stamped his feet at an ant that had run up his leg. He looked round reproachfully at Paul's endless delay.

"Ready, old chap! Just have to tie down the lids." Paul threw three or four saturated sacks over the tops of the drums and forced a couple of old cask lids down on top of them to prevent the water from spilling. His clothes were drenched from the splash and spill of the buckets and the constant runnels coursing down his arm and dribbling off the ends of his elbows. So he took off his shirt, wrapped it round his neck like a limp bandana, and pressed down his wide-brimmed hat as hard as he could. Then he had a last look round, took up the reins, and clicked his tongue.

"Righto! Let's go, Peter boy! Time to get moving."

The trolley lurched forward and they were on their way. It was exactly a quarter to nine.

CHAPTER FOUR

FROM the start of the return trip Paul was dismayed at the sluggish lurch of the trolley under the weight of the load. It was something he hadn't reckoned on. He had driven other vehicles on the station often enough—the Land-Rover, the truck, and most of all the rubber-tyred jinker—but all these had big rubber tyres that seemed to roll naturally and easily over any kind of surface. The unsprung trolley, with its narrow iron wheels that sank relentlessly into every patch of loose sand or dust, filled him with misgiving. The load, too, seemed unnaturally heavy until he paused to work it out. The water alone weighed eight hundred pounds, to say nothing of wet sacking and drums, lids, and thick wooden chocks; these, together with the trolley itself —the tray and the shafts, the axle-trees, axles, and wheels—were all dragging at poor Peter's shoulders. He resolved not to ride; he would walk every yard of the way, and even help if he could by pushing the load from behind.

Their first real test came at the Washaway. The trolley had lumbered sombrely down from the bore, groaning and creaking a little but still rolling freely enough. But as soon as it struck the bed of the creek it wallowed like a waterlogged raft. The channel was wide and flat—fifty or sixty yards of loose sand as dry

29

and fine as table salt—and the wheels seemed to sink and flounder about in it as helplessly as footprints swallowed in quicksand. Peter put his head down and strained forward on his shoulders. Paul could see the stamp of his forelegs and the quiver of his muscles as he pulled with all his power.

"Good boy, Peter! Good boy!" Paul cried encouragingly, pushing at the back of the trolley with one hand while he held the reins with the other. His contribution wasn't worth considering, but he liked to think it was as the load ploughed silently across the barren sand-bed and creaked up on to hard ground again. Behind them the wheel tracks had already turned into V-shaped ruts with sand-grains slipping down their loose walls as constantly and hopelessly as the scrabbling specks in an ant-lion's trap.

A yard or two further on stood a single coolibah, the last tree for four miles or more along the track, so Paul pulled up in its shade for a rest before the real onslaught began. He walked round the trolley, checking the pins in the axles and testing the firmness of the chocks holding the drums in place.

"All right, Peter! This is it, boy." He took up the reins again and they moved out across the plain. As soon as they left the shade of the tree the heat struck Paul in the face. He could feel the hot wind on his back and, although his skin was as brown as chocolate, he untied his shirt from his neck and slipped it over his shoulders again. With a shock he realized that it was dry already. Today was going to be a blisterer—one of those days that happened four or five times a year when the whole of the Centre was a furnace and the hollows shimmered like crucibles; when the temperature in the sandhills reached a hundred and thirty degrees and the sun was a welder's torch. He wondered whether he had made a mistake in attempting the trip on a day like this. Yet how was he to know what the weather would do? And wasn't it all the more vital to get through with the water now?

The trolley mumbled and lurched along. Much as he tried to avoid the humps and tussocks, Paul couldn't help striking them now and again. Then the whole tray tilted, and the water in the drums sloshed through the sacking and streamed from under the lids in waves and runnels that quivered down the sides of the drums and died away in dribbles through the wood. It fell in broad damp coins and wavering trails behind them, but so fierce were the sun and the greedy heat of the earth that the splatters of moisture faded before Paul's eyes and were gone as he watched. To him this spilling of water was like a haemorrhage, the loss of his own life-blood, but there was nothing he could do to stop it.

The sweat was gleaming on Peter's flanks when they reached the bottom of the Little Ridge. "Whoa!" Paul reined in to give him a rest, and studied the track ahead. He was uneasy. Although the dune was probably no more than fifty or sixty feet high, there were several treacherous stretches where the surface was as loose as beach sand. Nor was there any hope of avoiding them. Apart from the track itself the ridge was virgin land, covered with humps and obstacles enough to trap the trolley without hope of escape if once it bogged down there.

Paul climbed ahead for a short distance and studied the surface carefully. Then he returned and tied the reins loosely back on the trolley. It would be better, he decided, to lead the load himself. Although he knew that his own strength was useless when faced with a task like this, he unconsciously tensed himself as if he, too, was about to be put to the test.

"Now, Peter! Into it for all you're worth," he said, and taking him by the bridle he led off urgently to make a rolling assault on the ridge. Peter sensed the importance of the moment too, and the need to make a good start. He heaved violently at the load and almost ran at the incline with short fast steps.

"That's it! That's it, boy," Paul cried. "Keep her going." He knew how important it was to keep the wheels turning; the impetus of their forward motion could carry the trolley over the bad patches.

"Up, Peter! Up!" Their breath was coming in hard short gasps. The load, until now bumping along on an even keel behind them, canted backwards and suddenly became intolerably heavy. The water, tilting in the drums, sloshed over the back and ran down in a stream across the tray.

"Keep her going! Keep . . . her . . . going!" The wheels started to sink in the soft surface and they began to lose way. Peter was now pulling with every ounce of his strength. His back legs and haunches shook with the strain, his muscles bulged and roped from fetlock to wither. His nostrils flared and there was a wide glassy look of alarm, almost of panic, in his eyes as if he were terrified that this task was going to be too much for him. It wrenched Paul's heart to see it. Yet he couldn't give in. Not now. If once the trolley stopped they might never get it started again.

"Good . . . boy . . . Peter!"

They were more than half-way up. A few more minutes and the worst of the pinch would be over. Once on top of the ridge they could stop and rest as long as they wanted to; for, no matter how bad the surface might be on the other side, it was all downhill and the trolley would lunge its way forward without much effort.

Peter's breath was coming in hot gasps and his mouth spumed. He was almost at the end of his tether. Suddenly one of the front wheels lurched into a deep patch of loose sand and the whole trolley swung sharply. Peter staggered and all but lost his foothold.

"Look out!" It was an instinctive cry; the horse couldn't possibly understand the warning.

Paul dropped his hold on the bit and ran round to the back of the trolley, pushing and heaving with all his strength. For a foot or two more it ground onwards, but then, perhaps because Peter didn't understand Paul's sudden desertion and so slackened his effort for a second, perhaps because he was so utterly exhausted that he couldn't have driven himself on any further no matter what happened, he stopped in his tracks and the trolley stood still in the sand.

Paul came round to the side and leant against the tray, panting and drooping. They both stood in silence for a long time, Peter's flanks heaving and dripping with sweat. At last Paul got down on his hands and knees and smoothed away the sand in front of the wheels. He flinched as he did it, for already the ground was getting too hot to touch; in another hour it would be unbearable. He came round to the front again at last and stroked Peter comfortingly on the nose. "Sorry, boy," he said. "I didn't know it was going to be as tough as this."

He waited a little while longer until the panic left Peter's eyes, and the heaving of his flanks subsided. Then he took him by the bridle again. "Ready for another try? This time we'll shoot to the top." They were already three-quarters of the way up the slope. Another ten or twenty feet would see them to the crest. Paul braced himself. "Now, Peter!" he urged furiously. "Into it! Into it!" Peter seemed to double up with effort. He drove his forelegs down and heaved forward until the straining chains were as taut as hawsers. The wheels inched round slowly.

"That's it! That's it!" Paul cried. "She's coming." For a second or two it looked as if they might do it. The front wheels came out of the sand and the whole load steadied itself as it ground desperately forward. But then, just as they seemed to be gathering momentum again, the near-side wheels sank without warning. Peter staggered, checked himself, and then pulled strongly, but the more he tried, the deeper down he seemed to drive the iron tyres. As the whole load tilted sharply a sudden new danger loomed up before Paul.

"Stop! Stop!" he yelled, pulling back on the bridle. "It'll tip! The load'll tip!" He could picture the appalling catastrophe vividly in his mind—the tray tilted so far over that the two drums just slid off, tipping as they struck the edge and spilling all their water into the sand. It would be swallowed by the dune at a gulp.

"Whoa! Steady now! Easy! Easy!"

Gingerly he touched the near-side edge of the tray to test its stability. It seemed to be holding. As long as the wheels didn't sink any further the drums would remain upright. But there was no hope of pulling the trolley out as it was. The only way of bringing it back to an even keel was to dig away a trench for the off-side wheels as well, until they sank down to an even level with the rest.

He went round and squatted on his haunches as he started to dig and scrape with his hands. The ground was too hot for his bare knees, but by whipping off the surface sand as quickly as he could and digging down deeper he could just bear it. Before long he had hollowed out a long trench in front of the two off-side wheels. They stood up on two sandy knolls, ready to roll forward, Paul hoped, to even up the level of the load. He smoothed the sand as carefully as an old bush golfer working on a putting scrape until he felt confident that the load would move as he wished. It was hard work. The wind was blowing up to a full-scale northerly now, and it harried the loosened sand like beads of shot. Sometimes he had to shut his eyes and wait until the eddy and swirl subsided before he could go on.

Perhaps it was the chiselling edge of the wind that almost brought on tragedy again. Or perhaps it was a sudden movement from Peter, or the crumbling action of the sand. But just as Paul was reaching in as far as he could beneath the trolley it rolled forward without warning. The two off-side wheels slid down into the trench he'd made, and the whole load lurched back towards the right. He was flung on his back. The iron tyre of the back wheel drove the flesh of his upper arm against the sand, and for a sickening minute he thought he was pinned there permanently. Above him he saw the forward drum tilt. Panic seized him. If the drum rolled over it would fall directly down on him and crush him to death. He struggled violently, clawing and scraping with his fingers. Luckily his arm wasn't firmly caught—just a pinching of the flesh by the iron rim. He was free in a second, sitting up beside the trolley. But for a long time he was weak with fear.

If the wheel had rolled forward just a little further it would have gone over his arm, cracking the bones like sticks. And he would have lain there for hours in the heat, dying like a trapped fly in the sand.

He got up and looked at the load again. At least the trolley was level now, and the wheels rested firmly enough in the bottom of the trenches he'd scraped. The question was whether he'd really made a trap for himself, or whether once they had started they could gather enough momentum to pull the trolley out and keep it rolling onward to the top of the ridge. He knew one thing. The attempt would be vital—a last desperate try.

He went round and grasped Peter's bridle again. "Well, boy," he said. "This is it." He had decided it was better to lead from the front than to push from behind; at least each could see and understand what the other was doing.

"Ready now! One, two, three, *pull*!" They dug their feet in together, Paul straining with one hand on the bridle and the other hauling on the chain near the hames. "Pull, Peter, pull!" The trolley rolled forward slowly and uncertainly, three feet, five feet. . . .

"Not far now! Nearly there!"

But it was too much for them. Within a few yards of the top the wheels sank down again and, strain as he might, poor little Peter couldn't budge them. Wide-eyed and appalled he stood there in the shafts with his nostrils agape and his flanks heaving. His coat was caked with dirt and sweat, the hair—usually brushed and curry-combed with such care—matted and streaked and sticky, poking out in little points like the fibres of a badly washed paintbrush. Plainly he was saying "I'm done!"

Paul patted him on the nose. "It was a good try," he said. "You nearly did it." He surveyed their predicament. "And never mind about this mess. I'll think of something."

But what was he going to think of? It was all very well saying that, but how was it going to help? Paul leant against the tray of the trolley, shut his eyes and pressed his face into his hand. The wind was like a dragon's breath on his neck.

It was becoming a nightmare, this trip. A hellish journey through fire and suffering. Yet it had started out to be such a simple little thing. All he had wanted to do was to bring home a bit of water. But now it was becoming a life or death struggle, an agony of pain and frustration. Purgatory in the desert. He walked up to the crest of the ridge, so near that Peter's nose nearly touched it. Well, he wasn't going to give up. If this was a test, a journey for his spirit as well as his tired burnt body, then let it be. He'd get through with the water or die.

CHAPTER FIVE

THE first job, now, was to find something to put under the wheels. That was the root of the trouble. Where the surface was firm and hard they could trundle along quite easily, but loose sand was as deadly to them as glue to a fly. If only he had had the sense to think, he could have gone east for the water, to the Nullacoota Bore. It was nearly twice as far from the homestead, but over the whole distance the land was as flat as a table. Peter could have mooched along at his leisure.

But there was no point in thinking of that now. Here was the trolley bogged down in front of him and he had to get it out. He scouted round for something to bolster the track—grass, twigs, tussocks, bushes, anything to spread like matting and stop the wheels from sinking in. Suitable growth was hard to find, and it took him ten minutes or more to gather a couple of handfuls from the side of the slope. But the moment he started his tedding and spreading the wind whipped up the fragments and whirled them away over the crest of the dune like frightened birds. Paul pursed his lips. Even if he managed to gather another armful and weigh it down bit by bit with sand it would be an endless business. He could probably manage to get over the first ridge that way, but what of the Big Ridge beyond it. It would take him three hours to lay down a corduroy road over that great hump, even supposing he could collect enough brushwood and bed it all down.

He stopped on the ridge again and looked around. The north was a wall of dust. From far out over the Gidgicowie Plain brown clouds were billowing up; and beyond them again, far to the north and east, vast brown cliffs towered and wavered and spread across the sun. Nearer to him, almost at his feet, the surface of the plain was fountaining up in sudden bursts before the wind. Low driving clouds of dust were swept along, swooping and skimming from horizon to horizon. Even the Gidgee windmill, less than a mile away, was blurred and indistinct through the hot brown haze.

Yet the bore had the means to help him. It could break the deadlock of a loaded trolley caught in the grip of a sandhill. For there was iron at the bore—

sheets of old flat iron five or six feet long and perhaps a couple of feet wide, once used for covering the troughs, but long ago thrown aside and left to rust under the tank-stand. He had seen them there that morning. As usual, he hadn't been thinking, for if he had used his wits he would have loaded them on to the trolley. By now he could have laid down a track like a highway over the dunes.

He glanced at Peter again, standing there dejectedly in the heat with the wind whirling the sand in bursts like hail around his head. Poor Peter. He must be perishing of thirst, but there was no bucket on the trolley. Again Paul was angry with himself. What lack of foresight. Eighty gallons of water within a yard of Peter's tail, but not a drop for his parched tongue. It made Paul realize how thirsty he was himself. He climbed up on to the trolley, prised off one of the lids, and threw the sacking aside. Then he tilted back his hat, gripped the rim of the drum with his hands and, bending over until the tip of his nose tickled at the touch of the water, drank long and thirstily. Just as he finished, a wild gust of wind caught his hat and all but whisked it from his head. He threw up his hand and held it just in time. The familiar feel of the strong old felt with its wide brim suddenly gave him an idea. His father had often used it, according to old Moses, and so had most of the drovers.

The sight of Peter drooping in the shafts spurred Paul on. Without waiting to see if it leaked, Paul dipped his hat into the drum, let it fill with water, and then, descending gingerly from the trolley, carried it round to his friend. Peter slurped eagerly at the sudden miracle that had appeared in front of his nose. In six gulps the hat was empty. Paul went back for another hatful, then another and another. Five times he carried it round, brimming like a basin, before Peter was satisfied.

"That'll do for now," he said, patting Peter's wet nose. "It'll buck you up until I get back. Don't try to move, boy. I won't be long." He flicked open his leather watch-cover and looked at the time. "Gosh, I'd better not be. It's nearly eleven o'clock."

Peter turned his head and looked after him in alarm for a minute as Paul hurried off down the slope, but the stinging sand grains peppered his face until he turned to the front again and stood there stolidly and patiently with his shoulders hunched.

But if it was hard for Peter it was worse for Paul. All the way across the flat he had to fight his way against the wind and dust. It was like standing in front of the nozzle of a sanding gun. Swooping sheets of wind-harried sand stung his face, legs, and arms like the red-hot points of needles. He masked his face with his handkerchief and held up his arm to shield his eyes, but his legs went unprotected. Before long they were smarting and flecked with red spots like a bad rash of measles.

Stumbling and running, Paul arrived back at the bore at last and began to uncover the old sheets of galvanized iron that lay strewn about under the stones and bits of rotten timber. They were rusted and perforated in places, but still quite good for his purpose. He selected four of the best pieces and, pulling off a length of old fencing wire from a small roll under the stand, he bent it rapidly backwards and forwards until it snapped; then he tied one end of the wire to the sheets and the other in a loop round his waist. Since he knew it would be impossible to carry the iron in this wind he would drag it back to the trolley like a sledge. He broke off several more pieces of wire for emergencies and took up the old bucket he'd used in the morning. His face was wet with perspiration by the time he had finished, despite the fury of the wind. He went round to the troughs again and soused his face and arms. Then he took off his hat, filled it with water and poured it all over his head till his shirt and shorts were soaked. At least it made him feel better for a minute or two.

With the empty bucket in one hand and the loop of the towing wire in the other he started to drag his load back to the trolley. But he hadn't gone fifty yards when suddenly a great gust of wind lifted the four sheets of iron like petals and whirled them away. Luckily he hadn't yet looped the wire round his waist or he would have been flung off his feet and hurled about after them like a rag doll, with the edges of the iron chopping and gashing at him like huge knives. Instead, the sheets, still bound together, went flailing and cart-wheeling over and over like a flurry of wind-driven birds bursting into feathers and a mad tumble of beaks and wings.

Their flight was both a blessing and a disaster. Because of the angle of the wind the sheets were being carried off roughly in the direction of the ridge, and they were flinging along at a speed Paul could never have hoped for. He appeared to be getting his artificial trolley tracks dumped right in his lap. But how was he going to stop them without being cut to pieces? Moreover, once they were wrenched apart—and surely the wire couldn't hold them together much longer— there wouldn't be anything to prevent them from scattering far and wide over a million square miles of country from Broken Hill to the Great Australian Bight.

He broke into a run and set off in pursuit. Twice the iron paused in its flight and lay flat on the ground like a wilful pet lying doggo in a frolic of follow-the-leader. But each time it took off again before he could gather it up. Across the Washaway it hurtled, narrowly shaving the trees, though Paul was praying that it would wrap itself round the trunks or get caught in some of the branches. At last, a hundred yards from the ridge, it flopped for a minute in a lull, and Paul, panting along behind it, pounced and clung on. Then, though his face glistened and his breath came in gasps, he threaded another length of fencing wire through holes in the sheets at either end and bound them tightly. Locked together like this they formed an inert rectangle and he was able to drag them slowly up to the trolley.

Peter, who was flinching more than ever from the whip of the sand-grains round his flanks, was glad to see him again. Paul felt miserable at the sight of him; he had never intended that his best friend should be made to suffer like this. He took the bucket and climbed back on to the trolley to get him another drink. To his dismay he found the lids and sacking gone from the drums, stripped off by the wind and flung aside like scraps of straw. He could see one of the sacks lying caught in a tussock on the ridge, but there was no sign of the wooden lids, which had probably gone hurtling away like solid cartwheels.

Well, what was gone was gone; he would have to finish the trip with the water exposed to the sun and sky. But he salvaged the sacking, cut it into strips with his pocket knife, and wound it round his legs to protect them from the stinging sand. The remaining bits he used as gloves to guard his hands against the heat of the iron.

But though he now had a way of moving the trolley, he still had to put it to use. He had seen how violent and treacherous the sheets of iron could be in the wind, so he knew he had to use care and cunning. First he dragged the bundle to the side of the trolley, buried the end in the sand, and slowly untied the binding wire. Then, very quickly, he slid the topmost sheet forward and pushed it hard under the wheel as far as he could, heaping sand along the edges to keep it in place. He did the same thing on the other side, and then worked the two remaining sheets beneath and ahead of the first ones until he had a half hidden metal strip laid out over the worst part of the track. Finally, he went round to each wheel in turn, clearing away the heaped-up sand that the wind had already thrown there in eddying drifts.

"Well, boy," he said, taking Peter's bridle, "this is it. Now or never." He patted Peter's neck firmly once or twice with the palm of his hand, took a good grip, and pulled. "Up, boy! Up, boy! Into it! Into it!" Peter braced his feet and strained. "Pull, boy. Pull!" For a terrible second Paul feared that the trolley wasn't going to move at all; it seemed so solid and sluggish. "Pull, boy! Up! Up!" His voice suddenly rose in a note of triumph. "That's it! That's it! We've got him!" The wheels inched ahead, crunching slowly up on to the sheets of iron, and then rolled forward quickly and freely.

"Keep her going, Peter! Keep her going!" Paul was almost running, tugging encouragingly at the bridle, his face towards the load, his heels scuffing the sand as he plunged backwards up the ridge. Their momentum was enough to carry them over the crest. Although the wheels floundered and skewed about again as soon as they ran off the ends of the metal strip, there was no further danger of permanent bogging. Nor was Paul willing to give them a chance. Down the slope on the other side they went, lurching and swinging; Paul at the bridle leading and guiding quickly as the track veered and dipped; Peter pulling strongly as if anxious to get home after the blistering wait on the hill.

They left the sand at the bottom of the slope and ran out on to a good surface again in the dip between the two dunes, picking their way round tussocks and bumps on the loosely winding track, until the Big Ridge loomed up ahead. There, panting and red-faced, Paul called a halt. He tilted back his hat and ran his arm across his forehead. "That was a good run, boy! A real good run!"

He looked at his watch. It was almost midday.

CHAPTER SIX

But the most terrible part of the journey was still to come. The hollow between the two dunes was a crucible; the air was molten and fluid. Overhead, the sun hung as bare and inhuman as the lamp in an operating theatre. It was right at the zenith, burning down through a fiery aureole of dust. Ahead of them rose the cruellest obstacle of all—the Big Ridge. Not only was it higher and wider than the one they had just climbed, but the track wound about much more and ended in a sharp little pinch at the crest that would tax every ounce of their strength.

By now, too, they were both beginning to suffer from constant thirst and dehydration. It was like battling about in an oven. Paul crawled slowly on to the trolley. Although there was some shelter between the dunes from the main blast of the wind, it still whirled and buffeted about in swirling eddies.

Sometimes the sand and dust rose up in a sudden choking cloud and filled their ears and eyes and noses, even their mouths if they opened their parched lips for a second. Paul scooped aside the scum and bent his head to drink. The water was warm and gritty, almost undrinkable, but it soothed his lips at least and moistened his throat. He splashed his face and arms with it too, and soused his hair. Then he dipped a bucketful out of the other drum for Peter. The level there had already dropped by a third. If they kept on using the water at such a rate they'd barely have half of it left by the time they got home.

Peter drank greedily as usual and slurped at the bottom of the bucket when it was empty. Paul watched him pityingly. For everything depended on him—the safety of the poultry and pets, of Lily and Lena and old Moses, of Paul's two little sisters, of his own mother. In a way, the security of the whole homestead rested on the strength and wonderful willingness of one small horse. And because of it, Paul was afraid; afraid that the job was too big even for him, and that he would burst his heart trying to do it.

He hooked the bucket back on the trolley and went round to the front again. In one way or another this would be the end of the jagging and jolting of Peter's bit; once they reached the crest of the ridge he would go back to using the reins and they would rumble along to the homestead like a royal coach. For a moment he wondered whether he should go back for the sheets of iron and lay them down somewhere in advance, but he decided against it. It was better to see how far they could go without them; there would be time enough to drag them up if the trolley bogged down again.

"Well, Peter," he said, nuzzling the pony's nose against his shirt. "Now for the big one, eh?"

Peter bucked his head under Paul's armpit as he always did when he pretended to be impatient.

"All right," said Paul. "Ready? Try to get a good run at it if you can." He clicked his tongue and they moved forward. The surface was dusty but firm, and the iron wheels rolled out two smooth flat tracks that were scoured and swept by the wind as soon as the tyres had passed. They lumbered round the first curve in the slope, still moving freely, and started the stiff haul up the middle of the ridge. Now the real struggle began. As the strain grew, Peter plunged at the chains wildly. The look of panic returned to his eyes. Paul was certain that the little horse knew this was the final test and that he dared not fail in it.

Up they went. Half mad from the heat and dust, eyes smarting from sweat, flogged by the wind and sand, panting, slipping, struggling, they had only one purpose on earth—to keep the load moving. Alone there on the slope, strange and ungainly as an old-fashioned fire engine, the trolley and its two precious drums crept upwards; and all round them the whole continent ached in the heat. From horizon to horizon there was nothing but flying dust—no road, no fence, no life. Paul and his burden were alone in that vast solitude like a beetle on an unslaked waste of slag.

"Keep it up, boy!" Paul had to jerk the words out with his panting breath. "Keep . . . her . . . going! Keep . . . her . . . going!" Peter flailed with his feet, spreading them to gain more purchase as he strained, slipping and jerking, but always inching the trolley forwards and upwards. His flanks worked like bellows, and his nostrils flared.

"A bit further, boy? Can you get . . . a . . . bit . . . further?" They were more than half-way up. But the track was getting steeper and the surface worse. Paul knew they would have to halt for breath soon, but he was reluctant to give the word while they were still making headway. They were coming to a point where clumps of porcupine grass and tussocks dotted the track, and he was desperately trying to guide the trolley past them. Their pace had slowed to a crawl. Then, in attempting to steer all four wheels past the obstacles Paul swung the trolley slightly off the track; the off-side sank in sand and both front wheels slewed round harshly. Peter, pulling with the last gasps of his strength, was flung on to his knees. He struggled up, pawing and scrabbling with his forefeet, but it was too late. Their run had ended.

Paul stood by his friend for a long time, watching him heaving and panting, and comforting him with thanks and praise. More than anything he tried to shelter the poor animal's face and eyes. For the fury of the wind had reached its peak now, and up on the exposed slope of the Big Ridge it roared relentlessly. They couldn't exist here for long, Paul knew. The heat and wind, and their own exhaustion, would destroy them. Yet they hadn't much further to go. In another twenty or thirty yards they would reach the crest, and once over that they could travel the rest of the way with ease. They could even stop at the Tent Hills if they wanted to, and shelter in one of the caves for a while until they regained their strength. His mother would be getting worried by now, of course, but she knew he'd have enough sense to shelter from the sun on a day like this, at least until the wind dropped.

But first they must conquer the ridge. And it was obvious that there was only one way of doing that—the sheets of iron again. The portable road.

"Won't be long, boy." Paul left Peter hunched in his harness, and staggered off down the slope. He was beginning to feel light-headed and he knew that this was a sign of danger. But he wouldn't give in. He could have unhitched Peter, left the trolley where it was, and ridden home in half an hour. But that would have been surrender. He refused to consider it.

Across the dip he plodded, and up over the top of the Little Ridge until he came to the four sheets of iron still bent and half-buried in the sand where he had left them. Then there was the agony of gathering them up and binding them together again, and the final torture of hauling them back to the trolley. He had almost done it, stumbling along half dazed and senseless, when blood started running from his nose. He could feel it flowing down his upper lip through the sweat and dirt, and then he tasted it, warm and sickly, as it ran into his mouth. Big crimson drops fell on his shirt and knees. He wiped his arm across his lips and a long red smear spread from his elbow to his wrist.

Sobbing, choking, spattered with blood, he refused to give in. His nose had often bled before; it was common enough, he told himself, and nothing to worry about. But by the time he reached the trolley he was close to fainting. Little black darts were jabbing at his eyes like gnats, and there was a constant high-pitched ringing in his ears. He dropped down behind the trolley and just had the strength to crawl in beneath it and lie there in the shade on his back, swallowing the blood as it ran back down his throat. He lay there for what seemed an hour, with his hat pressed over his face, shielding it from the stinging lash of the wind. But in fact it was only for ten minutes. As soon as he felt the blood congeal and harden in his nostrils he crawled out again, clambered on to the trolley, and doused himself with water.

He had no handkerchief, but he soaked a piece of sacking and tied it round his forehead. For a few minutes trickles of water ran down his nose and cheeks, and he almost imagined they were cool. The bleeding stopped, but he now had to breathe through his mouth, and the heat and the dust dried out his throat like a kiln.

Their position was so critical that he knew he had to win through within a quarter of an hour or abandon the trolley altogether. Doggedly he dragged the iron forward and, using the same technique as before, pushed two of the sheets firmly under the front wheels. Then, in a calculated gamble, he went to set the other two in place at the base of the last little knoll, hoping to haul the load forward in an unbroken run. But he was unlucky. Before the last of the sheets could be bedded down it was caught by a sudden gust. With a crack like a gunshot it slammed up flat against the knoll and went cart-wheeling over the crest. There it took flight. For a second or two it spiralled up and then slowly, leisurely almost, it floated away high to the south like an old box-kite. Paul turned and trudged back to the trolley. He was stumbling a good deal now, becoming insensitive to accident and loss. But his will to succeed was as strong as ever.

"Easy now, boy," he said to Peter. "Just a short pull to get her started."

It was much harder than it sounded, but in the end they succeeded in getting the front wheels on to the edge of the iron. There they paused while Paul climbed up once more to dampen his face and ease his burning throat before making the final onslaught on the crest of the ridge. He was bending over the drum with his back to the gale when suddenly a violent gust struck him a punch between the shoulders. In a flash so quick that the reflexes in his arm were powerless his hat was whipped from his head. He flung up his hand despairingly, leapt from the trolley, and ran up the slope in pursuit. But in an instant he saw that it was hopeless. His hat was swept up over the rise and spun off across the plain at a speed no whippet could have matched. Long before Paul had toiled to the top of the dune the hat had been lost to sight in the wind-driven dust.

Now Paul knew that the crisis had really come. Without a hat in a place like this he could be struck down by sunstroke at any second like a pole-axed steer. He tore off his shirt, dampened it with water from the bucket, and wound it round his head like a turban. His bare back, he argued, could take the sun more readily than his bare head. But he was wrong. The stinging sand on his flesh was so unbearable that he screwed up his face with the pain. Plainly the idea was impossible. So he put his shirt back on again and un-wound the sacking from his legs. This he dipped in water and used as his turban instead; if some part of his body had to go naked, perhaps his legs could bear it best of all.

He was about to tie the bucket back on board when he paused. The bucket had suggested something to him. His position was desperate and time was critical. He would sacrifice some of the water as the price for succour.

The worst part of the track was the sharp pinch just below the crest of the ridge. Here the one sheet of iron that he'd been able to get into position would help him, but the loss of the other one left a treacherous patch of steep loose sand that two of the trolley wheels would have to traverse. That patch could mean disaster.

So Paul took the bucket, dipped it into the drum, and filled it with water; then he jumped down and carried the bucket to the danger spot. Here, quickly and carefully, he smoothed the sand and poured the water over it to consolidate it into a clear, firm surface. It needed three or four more bucketsful to cover the worst part of the strip, and even then Paul wondered whether the moisture had gone down deep enough to give the track some kind of foundation. But he dared not spare more. Already one drum was half empty, and every drop he poured out on to the sand was a loss that burnt into his hope and pride. It was not just a waste of water; it was a partial surrender, a compromise with defeat. He was selling his goal. Yet he argued that it was better to have something than nothing at all, better to bring home fifty gallons than none. He glanced quickly at the forlorn little strip already drying out before his eyes, and ran back to the trolley.

"Now, Peter," he said, gripping the bridle. "This is it." As usual, the little horse responded wonderfully, driving his feet downwards and backwards and heaving with his nuggety shoulders. Slowly, agonizingly, the front wheels crept up on to the iron strips. Then, suddenly, they rolled freely. Paul shouted encouragement, trying to seize his chance.

"That's it, Peter! Into it! Into it!"

The iron strips were so pitifully short that it was only a second or two before the wheels had gone forward on to sand again, but at least the smooth run had given the trolley some impetus. Everything now depended on the next few minutes. A couple of yards ahead lay the other iron sheet and the firm patch of damp sand. If they could keep the trolley moving until they reached this spot the struggle should be over.

"Pull, Peter! Pull!" There was no need for Paul to say it. Peter was pulling as if his life depended on it. Despite the dreadful nature of the surface and the steepness of the slope he hauled the load after him like an ox, jerking, ploughing, heaving, with the wheels carving wavering ruts behind them and the sand flying like seeds of shrapnel round his flanks.

"Nearly there, Peter! Nearly there!"

They had reached the worst part of the climb—the steep incline below the crest—and the trolley barely crept.

"A bit more! Just . . . a bit . . . more."

The load now hung back so heavily that it seemed impossible to go on. But at the last moment Peter seemed to sense something of Paul's desperation, the feeling that if they stopped they would never move the load again. He gave two or three convulsive heaves, the front wheels reached the firm surface, and the load suddenly rolled more easily again.

Up the pinch they went, higher and higher, until Peter's ears and nose began to rise over the top of the ridge and the whole sweep of dust-driven country opened out before them. But the trolley was still behind them on the slope and the final haul had still to come.

"Can you, Peter? Can you . . . do . . . it?" Paul's voice was a croaking whisper. "Just a few . . . feet . . . more?"

But it was the end. It came swiftly and suddenly. Just as they seemed to have victory within their grasp it was snatched away. For Peter had given up his last ounce of effort in that final pull, and when the trolley was ready to nose its way up over the crest he just didn't have the strength to do it. Worse still, he couldn't hold the load when once his forward run had ended. And at this point Paul's preparation of the surface, which was meant to be the turning point to their success, suddenly proved the greatest disaster of all.

For, in running back a foot or two, the loaded trolley began to skew sideways off the track; but while the off-side wheels still held firm on the sheet of iron, the rear wheel on the near-side slewed beyond the specially dampened strip and began to sink into the dry sand. The load immediately canted over. Paul saw the danger and cried out to Peter. "Hang on, boy! Hang on!" But it was a second or two before Peter could stop the backward drift; the tilt grew sharper because two wheels stood firmly on the iron while the other two sank deeper in the sand. Paul let go of the bridle and leapt round to try to check the sinking wheel.

"Hang on, boy, or she'll tip!" he yelled.

53

But he was an instant too late. Just as he reached the back of the trolley the rear wheel, teetering on the brink of a little ledge made by the roots of a tussock, rolled back over the edge and suddenly dropped four or five inches. Peter, his legs quivering from exhaustion, was thrown back momentarily by the jolt and slackened his pull. The tray of the trolley tilted dangerously, the weight of the load suddenly burst the wooden chocks aside, and the heavy drum slid down towards the sinking corner. It began slowly and ponderously like a juggernaut, but quickened its speed as it neared the end of the tray. Paul gave a wild cry and flung up his arms to check its slide, but it brushed him aside; then the bottom rim struck the edge of the tray, and the drum tipped forwards and plunged over the edge.

"No!" Paul screamed. "No! No! No!"

A waterfall curved out of the lidless drum for a second and gushed on to the sand. For an instant it flooded and seethed down the slope like slaking quick-lime and sank into the sand. Within five seconds nothing remained but an irregular splat of dampness on the hillside; the empty drum was still careering crazily down the dune.

For the first time in his life Paul gave in completely to despair. He sank down behind the trolley with his arms on his knees and his face buried against the bare flesh, trying to shut out the reality of the disaster.

"No!" he kept on repeating, half croaking, half sobbing. "No! No!"

But it was real, as real as the broiling sun overhead or the wind-ravaged plain or the scourge of the sand flogging his naked legs. And the pain of his

54

failure smarted and ached with reality more terrible than these, as if the land like an eagle had torn out his heart and laid it down bare under the torturing sun.

CHAPTER SEVEN

THE wind and the dust buffeted Paul back into action. No matter what his loss, he couldn't stay where he was. The height of the storm was approaching and he had to find shelter; he and Peter wouldn't survive much longer out here on the exposed crest of the dune in the full fury of the weather.

He climbed back on to the trolley and once more wet his face and neck. At the sight of the water he nearly broke down again; the one remaining drum was hardly half full, and the water which was warm and soupy, looked like the dregs of a mudhole. Moreover this was the stuff that he'd ladled out of the trough, so it would have to be boiled before it could be used by human beings. All the good water had gone into the sand with the capsized drum and had long since been gulped up by the ravenous wind.

Paul crawled down from the trolley and went round to take Peter's bridle again. He didn't even bother to look for the empty drum; it could lie in the desert and rot, or stare up vacantly at the sky as choked and lifeless as a mouth filled with sand.

"Come on, boy," he croaked. "Let's go home."

Even without the weight of the second drum Peter had a hard struggle getting the trolley out of the sand and hauling it over the crest of the ridge. But he did, with a furious, heart-bursting pull, and they started to coast down the other side. After the defeat and frustration of the ascent he seemed so eager to hurry home that Paul had to hold him back lest the trolley, plunging and skewing along behind him, should capsize altogether and spill out even the last miserable few gallons they'd salvaged.

The storm was closing in on them now like black daylight. An eerie gloom had spread across the sun, and dun-coloured cliffs of dust were shoring up the sky. Paul shivered, even in the gritty heat. There was something ominous and evil in the way the light was being snuffed out, even the immense power of the sun, choked and webbed round in skeins of dust a mile thick. It was like a midday eclipse, but worse. At least in an eclipse the sky still arched above the earth, high and firm, but now the sky and the earth were fused as one.

Paul had known dust-storms before, dozens of them, but never one so malignant as this. He began to suffer from a sense of claustrophobia, as if intangible blankets were closing in to stifle him; as if an invisible pad of dust as big as a paddock was about to be pressed against his face like dirty chloroform, muffling him firmly despite his struggling, until waves of darkness from the horizon slowly rolled over him.

He tugged at Peter's bridle. "Come on! Hurry, boy. The storm's coming up." They had come down the leeward slope of the Big Ridge and were shambling along towards the line of tent hills a mile away to the south. The track, though level now, grew rougher as they went, until the drum boomed constantly as the trolley rattled over the gibbers. A weird and terrifying setting it was, with the dark walls of the storm all round, the grim outline of Old Table Top ahead, and the half-empty drum booming and knelling through the murk like a lost spirit. As they entered the pass through the line of tent hills the light grew gloomier than ever. They were still more than two miles from the homestead, and visibility had dropped to nothing.

"Have to stop and take shelter," Paul said. "Might get bushed on the Flat in this light; then where would we be?" He led Peter off the track for a little way on the leeward side of Old Table Top until he came to a small quarry where his grandfather had excavated slabs of stone long ago when he'd first built the station homestead.

"Not much of a place, boy, but it's better than nothing." He unhitched the straps and chains, lowered the shafts, and led Peter round to the back of the trolley. "At least there's shelter from the wind." Then he clipped the bridle to the tray and climbed up to get a bucket of water. Again Peter drank noisily, nuzzling the bottom of the bucket for more.

"Don't know how you can stomach the stuff," Paul said. "But you can have one refill." He gave it to him and then tied the bucket back on to the trolley. "Now you stay here and have a good rest," he said, patting his friend's neck. "I'm going up to the caves until the worst of the storm clears."

Peter's gaze followed him for the first few yards, but the little pony was so exhausted that his head soon drooped and he stood there silent and motionless, grateful for the rest after his hellish struggle.

Paul climbed slowly up the face of Old Table Top, his lips and throat burning. He desperately wanted a drink, but he hadn't brought any matches so there was no hope of boiling any water from the drum. He consoled himself with the thought that the old bucket on the trolley leaked so badly that he couldn't have boiled water in it anyway; and that even if he had, it would have taken hours to cool.

As he climbed on, little patches of scree sometimes slid away beneath his feet, bringing him to his knees. Once a fairly large stone, dislodged by his slipping foot, went tumbling down the slope, and he quickly veered away to the left to avoid bringing down an avalanche of rock on poor Peter's head.

At last, a couple of hundred feet up, he came to the edge of the breakaway, the sudden sheer cliff face where the hard capping of the old table top ended abruptly. And there, in ragged line, were the caves that from time immemorial had looked out over the Munlacowie Plain from the ancient world of the aborigines.

Panting and exhausted, his forehead wet under the ragged hessian fringe of his crude hat, his face smeared with dried blood and dirt, and his bruised side seared by a dark red weal, Paul must have looked just like a wounded warrior crawling up for refuge in the tribal caves under the totems of his ancestors. Behind him, and all around on the rock faces and in the wind-worn niches, the ancient carvings and drawings stood still and watched him. And he, Paul Anderson, on the first great trial of his initiation into manhood, sank down exhausted at the mouth of the cave, leaned his head back gratefully against the rock, and closed his eyes.

Before him he could have seen nothing, because there was nothing to see. The horizon had ceased to exist; the vast stretch of the Munlacowie Plain, the homestead itself, even the creek—less than two miles ahead of his gaze—were all blotted out in the darkness of the dust. A boy might wander there for days without a landmark, perishing at last with his mouth pressed to this hard hot land and his lips parched with her kiss.

But behind him, in the cave, his closed eyes were free to see. And there was amazement on his face when the tussocks above him on Old Table Top clicked together with the sound of old bones, and the wind mourning round the breakaway moaned and droned with the chant of didgeridoos. For a moment his blood ran cold, and his warm heart was squeezed by a hand of ice; for out of the cave, out of the darkness, came whole generations and centuries of men. The ancient dancers came down from the walls, glowing white with ochre like phosphorus in the night, posturing gravely round him as he sat there with his head against the stone, the red weal down his side and the blood on his hands. They threw up their arms and moved round him and through him, their motions always sedate and slow to the music of the wind playing on the didgeridoo of the hill.

And there were creatures, too, that crawled down from the cliffs of the walls—claw-toed goannas with jaws like shovel heads, geckos and frills and skinks, all painted yellow and orange and white, with ochre markings over their bodies and straight lines and patterns picked out on the flat slates of their backs and the clean curves of their bellies.

There were emus too, strange three-toed emus with white ochre legs that glowed like skeletons; and kangaroos with looped tails curved ready to whack the ground. The kangaroos leapt down from their places and fled into the caves, with hunters as white as bones stalking after them, notching the long bloodwood spears in the cradle of their woomeras and gazing fiercely out of the walls with eyes like gimlets. And out of the dark came strange and terrible creatures too, floundering from the mud of the past like hippopotamuses bellowing up at Old Table Top from their vast faraway graves at Callabonna and Lake Eyre, forever mourning their own extinction in those great vats of salt.

And through it all, breaking over Paul in waves of fear and terror, shaking the hills and driving the scurrying hunters before it like dust in the wind, came the bull-roarer wail of the bunyip. All the white-ochre dancers froze at the sound, their bones aglow in the gloom, posed in weird attitudes until the terrible cry passed by and went echoing away down the creeks of the past. Then the wind blew more loudly on its didgeridoo and the dancers moved out again.

And now the corroboree quickened all round Paul. Over and through the rock of his body the bone-white figures flew, thumping their feet in a frenzy. The storm above them clicked the sticks of the bushes together more wildly, and the animals fled through the shadows like the frieze on a merry-go-round. The walls of the caves began to spread and grow, towering far above him, until suddenly they were one with the sky. And the creatures had all the world to roam in; the goannas and skinks raced far down the side of the sky, the emus ran endlessly on, and at one bound the kangaroos leapt to the further-most edge of the plain. The dancers whirled more furiously than ever, the sticks clicked more sharply, and the note of the wind in the didgeridoo rose higher and grew louder.

Suddenly the whole hillside was shaking. The dancers threw themselves down on their faces with terror and the animals propped, motionless. For the Rainbow Serpent had started to move in the mountain. His scales rasped on the underground rocks, and his coils heaved like thunder. It seemed as if the whole hilltop was bursting open and the world was alight with white fire.

Paul cried out and jumped to his feet. Behind him the ochre-coloured dancers stood stock still, the hunters held back their spears, the animals froze on the stone. Ahead, through the open mouth of the cave, the world was deep in gloom until, again, the weird landscape in the sky was lit up by a flash as white as naphtha, as sharp as a magnesium flare. Paul winced and blinked. It was lightning.

And now, for half an hour after his dream, he watched the storm light up the fantastic country of the sky, rubbing his eyes at the dazzling glare of each flash. The wind was dropping and the dust hung in bays and promontories above him, billowing slowly and changing contours like fluid continents, melting, perishing and emerging reborn as they drifted away to the south.

The storm centre, towards which the burning wind had raged all day, was passing rapidly south-eastwards. Thunder and lightning were there, racing and crashing along the edge of the monsoon front; and perhaps a little rain. But to the parched Inland it was just another dry thunderstorm; the land might crouch as expectantly as it pleased, the coolibahs along the creek might lift up their branches in supplication, but on

Munlacowie Station there would be no rain today.

Paul tried to look at his watch, but he couldn't see anything in the gloom. He sensed that it was long after sunset. Four or five hours at least must have passed since he'd climbed up to the cave and, exhausted and light-headed, slumped down there with his back to the stone.

A puff of cool air came through the mouth of the cave and fanned his face. The wind was changing. In another hour the cool breeze from the south would have established itself and driven much of the dust eastwards. Already the sky was beginning to clear a little, and the moon was coming through in a milky stain. It was time to go home.

Home! The thought shot through his half-delirious mind. His mother! What agony had she gone through this day, eyes constantly straining through the rising wind and dust for signs of his own return, ears alert for radio news of his father's crisis. What must she still be suffering now? For he, Paul, hadn't returned. Not by nightfall. Not even yet.

A great wave of pity and sadness, remorse, and frustration, struck Paul. It mingled with the pain in his side and the aching smart in his back and his arms, until it shook him like a sob. He wiped his knuckles across the lower lids of his eyes; they were wet when he brushed the back of his hand against his shirt.

"You were right, Mum." Outwardly to the lonely desolation round him the words went unsaid, but they ached in his heart and formed on his lips. His mother —quiet, gentle, not really brave but endlessly patient and warm-hearted—had been made to suffer again. Was still suffering. And as usual by his own pride and self-confidence. By heeding her advice, by admitting defeat earlier, he could have spared her much suffering, and saved himself and poor Peter needless agony. But he was headstrong and confident and stubborn. And he was almost a man.

Hastily he scrambled down the slope and made his way back to the trolley.

CHAPTER EIGHT

THE slope down the side of Old Table Top was steep and treacherous. It had been bad enough by day-light—or dust-light, as Paul's father would have called it—but it was worse now. The vague translucence of the moon was barely enough to mark out the bigger humps and hollows; the loose patches of scree and the hard, melon-sized stones flung down from the breakaway above, were hidden in shadow. A false step now, a sudden twist or trip, and his ankle could break with a crack like a snapped carrot. And then how long might he lie on the side of the barren old mesa before search parties found him.

Yet Paul took no notice of this, not even the sickening slide of the talus suddenly giving way be-neath his feet and carrying him down helplessly towards the edge of the quarry. For somehow he managed to crawl across the face of the slope like a spider whenever danger threatened, and so, zigzagging slowly, he eventually made his way to the bottom. He felt no fear. Perhaps he was still half delirious, or rapt in the memory of the silent death-dance of the aboriginal figures on the hill. Perhaps he had even joined them, and was now only stepping out of his white painted skeleton on the wall of the cave to go stalking game on the hillside through the silver murk of the moon.

But Peter's whinny and his sharp velvety sneeze in the night brought back the present again. He was standing by the trolley, snorting the tickle of dust out of his nostrils and stamping impatiently. The passing storm and the cool sweep of the new breeze had roused him, and he was anxious to set off for home.

"Coming," Paul shouted, picking his way round the broken edges of the quarry. "No need to stamp and fuss." He reached the trolley and rubbed Peter's nose. "Hullo, boy. Lonely, eh?" He pushed the pony's ears in under his armpit. "Well, we'll be on the track in a second." Paul took the bucket and climbed on to the trolley. "Must have a drink first." He dipped the bucket far down into the drum for water. "Have to. Got a throat like a pepper-pot."

There was only a foot of dirty water left in the bottom of the drum, but he managed to ladle some of it out and lifted the whole bucket clumsily to his lips. The water swilled and spilt down his chin and ran in a stream from his elbows. He panted and blew as he drank.

"Ah-h!" he said at last, setting down the bucket in front of Peter's nose. "Hydatids or no hydatids, I needed something wet to put out the fire on my tongue." He listened in silence for a moment to the sound of Peter's drinking. Then he put aside the bucket and harnessed the horse back in the trolley again.

Now, for the first time on that terrible homeward journey, Paul rode on the trolley and guided Peter with the reins. They skirted the eerie arc round the bottom of the hill until they intercepted the vague scrabble of the track; then they struck out for home.

Suddenly Paul was cold. Under his thin, sleeveless shirt, damp from the dribbling bucket, his skin was a prickle of goose-flesh. And in his ears the wheels bumped and the drum boomed, and the blurred moon-scape quivered and jolted before his eyes. For a minute the directions spun on the plain, time drained away and they were rumbling and rattling through the grey dawn of the morning to fill their load at the Gidgicowie Bore. But then the track lurched, the compass swung, and the night brought back the sick moon across their homeward march again. A line of black mushrooms rose out of the ground ahead, and stalked motionlessly over the plain towards them. And when at last the dark shapes moved past them the rumbling of the trolley was suddenly snuffed into silence and Peter was struggling to haul his load through the dry sand of the creek bed. Munlacowie Creek, and the dark line of its straggling coolibahs! They were nearly home.

The drag of the load was heavy and slow in the creek. Paul jumped from the trolley to help, and his feet sank into sand again. That feeling of sand! It was burnt into his soul. That strange gritty rub at each step, that chafe on the toes, that exhausting slip backwards as he walked. . . . He would feel it under his feet till he died.

Peter panted and struggled to reach the homeward bank. In the end they crossed their river of dust, steered painfully over that last soft waterway of sand, and came out on to the homestead plain. And there, before them, was home. Peter called up the flagging muscles of his poor racked body and almost quickened his pace. Paul opened his cracked lips and let out a home-coming croak. And the almost empty water drum rumbled its droll warning of their coming.

As they came trudging up to the houseyard gate, Paul suddenly saw a light burst on the veranda and his mother came running down the yard.

"Paul! Paul!"

"It's all right! It's me, Mum!" His voice was a whispered croak. He had meant it to sound off-hand and light-hearted, but it came out like a corncrake's.

"Paul, are you all right?"

"Yeah! Got caught in the storm. Sorry I'm late."

She had reached him now and clutched him in her arms tightly, unconsciously, ignoring his words and the panting of her own voice as she repeated over and over again in a kind of agony of relief, "Thank God, Paul! Thank God! Oh, thank God!" He was overwrought himself, bodily rather than emotionally, and stood there helplessly until she had finished.

"Quite a . . . quite a trip," he said at last, inanely. "Poor old Peter. Nearly done in."

It was the relief they both sought. "Better unharness him. Poor fellow." And Paul stumbled from his mother's embrace and started to unhitch the shafts. His mother helped him with quick, deft hands; then they sent Peter off to the yards and went up to the house. He was glad she hadn't looked in the drum or asked about the water.

"Had to shelter. . . ." he said jerkily. "Up in the breakaway. Storm was pretty bad."

She hadn't really heard a word. "Look at you! Oh, Paul, just look at you." They had entered the kitchen and Paul flopped down on the bench by the table. She kept gazing at him in relief and unbelief and didn't really take in what she saw. Burnt and bloodshot, his hair and nostrils thick with dust, lips cracked, face smeared and scratched, he had stepped right out of the history of her imagination—a small replica of those giant explorers who brooded for ever over Australia's heart.

"Sorry we didn't get much water, Mum," he said. "Only half a drum." Even at the end, for his pride's sake, he had to snatch that little lie. He knew there was barely a foot of water left—ten gallons, perhaps, of soupy muck. But failure was hard to announce, even to himself.

"We lost a drum in the storm."

She was busying herself with food, strangely unable to look at him. "Paul! You're back!" She cleared her throat and seemed to need the tea-towel near her face. "No need to worry about water." She brightened artificially. "We'll live on preserves for a week if we have to; drink jars full of fruit juice and syrup."

And to Paul, suddenly slobbering over a brimful basin of apricot syrup, no food or drink could have sounded cooler or sweeter. He grinned grotesquely with his cracked lips. "Wash in it too, can we?"

When he'd finished he stumbled off to his room. Unwashed. His mother followed him. "Better get some sleep, Paul. And don't get up in the morning." Silly comment, she thought to herself. Silly, unnecessary comments, just for the sake of talking. For they both knew there were things not made for words.

"Any news of Dad?"

"Not since this morning. The radio's dead."

"The storm I s'pose."

"Probably."

"What did they say this morning?"

"Nothing. They didn't know."

" 'Bout time they did."

She drew a white sheet over his sun-blackened back. "Maybe we'll hear tomorrow. Perhaps it'll be good news."

"Hope so."

"Now get some rest."

"Gosh, yes. Beaut, the feel of the sheets."

He closed his eyes, and straightaway sluggish black waves lifted him up and started to carry him off through the wall. His mother stood silently watching him, sensing even in his imminent sleep the strange meaning of his journey. As she looked down she could feel the ache of his flesh, the cruel exhaustion of his body, and because she was his mother she understood.

He had gone out in the morning for two drums of fresh water, and he had come back with a dishful of sludge; he had gone out confident and strong and come back stumbling and ashamed; he had gone out a boy, but he was a boy no longer. For a whole day a continent had hurled itself at him, and he had beaten it back.

Outside, she could hear the southerly moving in the eaves and knew that the dust would be rolling away and the moonlight spreading wanly across the vast plains of the Inland. Loneliness, solitude, isolation!

So Paul had had his Pyrrhic victory and they had both learnt something. In the end it wasn't things that mattered. It was man. In spite of radio or Flying Doctor planes, jet engines or Woomera's signposts to space not far away, men were still measured by the elemental things—by food, water, shelter. And the strength of

68

their own spirit. That was what mattered. The will to go on. Perhaps some day they would have to survive on that alone. As Paul had today.

She tidied the tea-towels and put out the light. On the way down the passage she paused at his door and shone the torch in on his bed. He lay quite still. Everything did. The room, the house, the homestead, the whole world. In darkness and solitude the terrible sense of their isolation swept in on her again as she stood watching him. No news had come through to them, no hint of help. If his father lay dying at this moment they could not know. And yet intuitively she knew that she would survive as Paul had done. Body racked, spirit annealed, he lay sprawled on the bed, his arms flung forward like someone fallen in battle, his head pressed sideways into the pillow.

And he slept.

Storm Boy

Storm Boy lived between the South Australian Coorong and the sea. His home was the long, long snout
of sandhill and scrub that curves away south-eastwards from the Murray Mouth. A wild strip it is,
windswept and tussocky, with the flat shallow water
of the Coorong on one side and the endless slam of
the Southern Ocean on the other. They call it the
Ninety Mile Beach. From thousands of miles around
the cold, wet underbelly of the world the waves come
sweeping in towards the shore and pitch down in a
terrible ruin of white water and spray. All day and all
night they tumble and thunder. And when the wind
rises it whips the sand up the beach and the white
spray darts and writhes in the air like snakes of salt.

Storm Boy lived with Hideaway Tom, his father.
Their home was a rough little humpy made of wood
and brush and flattened sheets of iron from old tins.
It had a dirt floor, two blurry bits of glass for windows,
and a little crooked chimney made of stove pipes
and wire. It was hot in summer and cold in winter,
and it shivered when the great storms bent the sedges
and shrieked through the bushes outside. But Storm
Boy was happy there.

Hideaway was a quiet, lonely man. Years before,
when Storm Boy's mother had died, he had left
Adelaide and gone to live like a hermit by the sea.
People looked down their noses when they heard about
it, and called him a beachcomber. They said it was a
bad thing to take a four-year-old boy to such a wild,

lonely place. But Storm Boy and his father didn't mind. They were both happy.

People seldom saw Hideaway or Storm Boy. Now and then they sailed up the Coorong in their little boat, past the strange wild inlet of the Murray Mouth, past the islands and the reedy fringes of the fresh-water shore, past the pelicans and ibises and tall white cranes, to the little town with a name like a water-bird's cry—Goolwa! There Storm Boy's father bought boxes and tins of food, coils of rope and fishing lines, new shirts and sandals, kerosene for the lamp, and lots of other packages of this and that, until the little boat was loaded to the brim.

People in the street looked at them wonderingly and nudged each other. "There's Tom," they'd say, "the beachcomber from down the coast. He's come out of his hideaway for a change." And so, pretty soon, they had just nicknamed him "Hideaway," and nobody even remembered his real name.

Storm Boy got his name in a different way. One day some campers came through the scrub to the far side of the Coorong. They carried a boat down to the water and crossed over to the ocean beach. But a dark storm came towering in from the west during the day, heaving and boiling over Kangaroo Island and Cape Jervis, past Granite Island, the Bluff, and Port Elliot, until it swept down towards them with lightning and black rain. The campers ran back over the sand-hills through the flying cloud and the gloom. Suddenly one of them stopped and pointed through a break in the rain and mist.

"Great Scott! Look! Look!"

A boy was wandering down the beach all alone. He was as calm and happy as you please, stopping every now and then to pick up shells or talk to a petrel standing forlornly on the wet sand with his wings folded and his head pointing into the rising wind.

"He must be lost!" cried the camper. "Quick, take my things down to the boat; I'll run and rescue him." But when he turned round the boy had gone. They couldn't find him anywhere. The campers rushed off through the storm and raised an alarm as soon as they could get back to town:

"Quick, there's a little boy lost way down the beach," they cried. "Hurry, or we'll be too late to save him." But the postmaster at Goolwa smiled. "No need to worry," he said. "That's Hideaway's little chap. He's your boy in the storm."

And from then on everyone called him Storm Boy.

The only other man who lived anywhere near them was Fingerbone Bill, the aboriginal. He was a wiry, wizened man with a flash of white teeth and a jolly black face as screwed-up and wrinkled as an old boot. He had a humpy by the shore of the Coorong about a mile away.

Fingerbone knew more about things than anyone Storm Boy had ever known. He could point out fish in the water and birds in the sky when even Hideaway couldn't see a thing. He knew all the signs of wind and weather in the clouds and the sea. And he could read all the strange writing on the sandhills and beaches—the scribbly stories made by beetles and mice and bandicoots and ant-eaters and crabs and birds' toes and mysterious sliding bellies in the night. Before long Storm Boy had learnt enough to fill a hundred books.

In his humpy Fingerbone kept a disorganized collection of iron hooks, wire netting, driftwood, leather, bits of brass, boat-oars, tins, rope, torn shirts, and an old blunderbuss. He was very proud of the blunderbuss because it still worked. It was a muzzle-loader. Fingerbone would put a charge of gunpowder into it; then he'd ram anything at all down the barrel and fix it there with a wad. Once he found a big glass marble and blew it clean through a wooden box just to prove that the blunderbuss worked. But the only time Storm Boy ever saw Fingerbone kill anything with it was when a tiger-snake came sliding through the grass to the shore like a thin stream of black glass barred with red-hot coals. As it slid over the water towards his boat Fingerbone grabbed his blunderbuss and blew the snake to pieces.

"Number One bad fellow, tiger-snake," he said. "Kill him dead!" Storm Boy never forgot. For days afterwards every stick he saw melted slowly into black glass and slid away.

At first, Hideaway was afraid that Storm Boy would get lost. The shore stretched on and on for ninety miles, with every sandhill and bush and tussock like the last one, so that a boy who hadn't learnt to read the beach carefully might wander up and down for hours without finding the spot that led back home. And so Hideaway looked for a landmark.

One day he found a big piece of timber lying with the driftwood on the beach. It had been swept from the deck of a passing ship, and it was nearly as thick and strong as the pile of a jetty. Hideaway and Fingerbone dragged it slowly to the top of the sandhill near the humpy. There Hideaway cut some notches in the wood for steps, and fixed a small cross-piece to it.

Then they dug a deep hole, stood the pole upright in it, and stamped it down firmly.

"There," said Hideaway. "Now you'll always have a lookout post. You'll be able to see it far up the beach, and you won't get lost."

As the years went by, Storm Boy learnt many things. All living creatures were his friends—all, that is, except the long, narrow fellows who poured themselves through the sand and sedge like glass.

In a hole at the end of a burrow under a grassy tussock he found the Fairy Penguin looking shyly at two white eggs. And when the two chicks hatched out they were little bundles of dark down as soft as dusk.

"Hullo, Mrs Penguin," said Storm Boy each day. "How are your bits of thistle-down today?"

Fairy Penguin didn't mind Storm Boy. Instead of pecking and hissing at him she sat back sedately on her tail and looked at him gently with mild eyes.

Sometimes in the hollows behind the sandhills where the wind had been scooping and sifting, Storm Boy found long, white heaps of sea-shell and bits of stone, ancient mussels and cockles with curves and whorls and sharp broken edges.

"An old midden," said Hideaway, "left by the aborigines."

"What's a midden?"

"A camping place where they used to crack their shell-fish." Fingerbone stood for a long time gazing at the great heaps of shells, as if far off in thought.

"Dark people eat, make camp, long time ago," he said a little sadly. "No whitefellow here den. For

74

hundreds and hundreds of years, only blackfellows."

Storm Boy looked at the big heaps of shell and wondered how long ago it had been. He could paint it in his mind . . . the red camp-fires by the Coorong, the black children, the songs, the clicking of empty shells falling on the piles as they were thrown away. And, he thought to himself, "If I had lived then, I'd have been a little black boy."

But his father's voice roused him and he ran down to the beach to help dig up a bagful of big cockles for their own tea. When they had enough for themselves they filled more bags to take up to Goolwa, because there the fishermen and the tourists were eager to pay Hideaway money for fresh bait.

Storm Boy stood bent over like a horse-shoe, as if he were playing leap-frog; his fingers scooped and scraped in the sand, and the salt sea slid forwards and backwards under his nose. He liked the smell and the long smooth swish of it. He was very happy.

Storm Boy liked best of all to wander along the beach after what Hideaway called a Big Blow. For then all kinds of treasure had been thrown up by the wind and the wild waves. There, where the wide stretch of beach was shining and swishing with the backward wash, he would see the sea-things lying as if they'd been dropped on a sheet of glass—all kinds of weed and coloured kelp, frosty white cuttlefish, sea-urchins, and star-fish, little dead sea-horses as stiff as starch, and dozens of different shells—helmets, mitres, spindles, and dove-shells, whelks with purple edges, ribbed and spiral clusterwinks, murex bristling out their frills of blunt spines, nautilus as frail as frozen foam, and sometimes even a new cowrie, gleaming and polished, with its underside as smooth and pink as tinted porcelain.

In places the sand would be wrinkled and puckered into hard smooth ripples that looked like scales. Storm Boy liked to scuff them with his bare soles as he walked, or balance on their cool curves with the balls of his feet.

Storm Boy grew up to be supple and hardy. Most of the year he wore nothing but shorts, a shirt, and a battered old Tom Sawyer hat. But when the winter wind came sweeping up from Antarctica with ice on its tongue, licking and smoothing his cheeks into cold flat pebbles, he put on one of his father's thick coats that came down to his ankles. Then he would turn up the collar, let his hands dangle down to get lost in the huge pockets, and go outside again as snug as a penguin in a burrow. For he couldn't bear to be inside. He loved the whip of the wind too much, and the salty sting of the spray on his cheek like a slap across the face, and the endless hiss of the dying ripples at his feet.

For Storm Boy was a storm boy.

Some distance from the place where Hideaway and Fingerbone had built their humpies, the whole stretch of the Coorong and the land around it had been turned into a sanctuary. No one was allowed to hurt the birds there. No shooters were allowed, no hunters with decoys or nets or wire traps, not even a dog.

And so the water and the shores rippled and flapped with wings. In the early morning the tall birds stood up and clapped and cheered the rising sun. Everywhere there was the sound of bathing—a happy splashing and sousing and swishing. It sounded as if the water had been turned into a bathroom five miles long, with thousands of busy fellows gargling and gurgling and blowing bubbles together. Some were above the water, some were on it, and some were under it; a few were half on it and half under. Some were just diving into it and some just climbing out of it. Some who wanted to fly were starting to take off, running across the water with big flat feet, flapping their wings furiously and pedalling with all their might. Some were coming in to land, with their wings braking hard and their big webbed feet splayed out ready to ski over the water as soon as they landed.

Everywhere there were criss-crossing wakes of ripples and waves and splashes. Storm Boy felt the excitement and wonder of it; he often sat on the shore all day with his knees up and his chin cupped in his hands. Sometimes he wished he'd been born an ibis or a pelican.

But sometimes Storm Boy saw things that made him sad. In spite of the warnings and notices, some people did hurt the birds. In the open season, shooters came chasing wounded ducks up the Coorong; some sneaked into the sanctuary during the night, shot the birds at daybreak, and crept out again quickly and secretly. Visitors went trampling about, kicking the nests and breaking the eggs. And some men with rifles, who called themselves *sportsmen*, when unable to find anything else to shoot at, bet one another that they could hit an egret or a moor-hen or a heron standing innocently by the shore. And so they used the birds for target practice. When they hit one they laughed and said, "Good shot!" and then walked off leaving it lying dead with the wind ruffling its feathers. Sometimes, if it wasn't too far away, they walked up to it, turned it over with their feet and then just left it lying there on its back.

When Storm Boy ran back to tell his father about it, Hideaway muttered angrily, and Fingerbone slapped his loaded blunderbuss and said, "By yimminy, I fill him with salt next time! If dem fellows come back, *boom*, I put salt on their tails."

When Storm Boy laughed at that, Fingerbone flashed his white teeth and winked at Hideaway. Neither of them liked to see Storm Boy looking sad.

When Storm Boy went walking along the beach, or over the sandhills, or in the sanctuary, the birds were not afraid. They knew he was a friend. The pelicans sat in a row, like a lot of important old men with their heavy paunches sagging, and rattled their beaks drily in greeting; the moor-hens fussed and chattered; the ibises cut the air into strips as they jerked their curved beaks up and down; and the blue crane stood in silent dignity like a tall thin statue as Storm Boy went past.

But one morning Storm Boy found everything in uproar and confusion. Three or four young men had gone into the sanctuary. They had found some pelican nests—wide, rough nests of sticks, grass, and pelican feathers as big as turkey quills—and they had killed two of the big birds nesting there. After that they had scattered everything wildly with their boots, kicking and shouting and picking up the white eggs and throwing them about until they were all broken. Then they had gone off laughing.

Storm Boy crept forward in fear and anger. From behind a tussock he looked round sadly at the ruin and destruction. Then, just as he was about to run back to tell Fingerbone to fill his blunderbuss with salt, he heard a faint rustling and crying, and there under the sticks and grass of the broken nests were three tiny pelicans—still alive. Storm Boy picked them up carefully and hurried back to Hideaway with them.

Two of the baby pelicans were fairly strong, but the third was desperately sick. He was bruised and hurt and helpless. He was so weak that he couldn't even hold up his head to be fed; he just let it drop back flat on the ground as soon as Storm Boy or Hideaway let go of it.

"I don't think he'll live," said Hideaway. "He's too small and sick."

Even old Fingerbone shook his head. "Dem bad fellows kill big pelican. Don't think little fellow stay alive now."

"He mustn't die," Storm Boy said desperately. "He mustn't! He mustn't!"

He wrapped up the tiny bruised body in one of Hideaway's scarves, and put it by the fire. All day long he watched it lying there, sometimes moving feebly or opening its beak to give a noiseless little cry. Every now and then he poured out a drop of cod-liver oil from the bottle that Hideaway had once bought for him, and tried to trickle it down the baby bird's throat.

Night came on, and still Storm Boy watched the sick little fellow hour after hour, until Hideaway spoke firmly about bed and sleep. But Storm Boy couldn't sleep. Again and again through the night he slipped out of bed and tip-toed across the dirt floor to the fireplace to make sure the baby pelican was warm enough.

And in the morning it was still living.

It was three days before the baby pelican was well enough to sit up and ask for food. By then his two brothers had their beaks open hungrily all the time, although of course they were still too young to have their creels or fishing baskets ready.

"Anyone would think that I was Grandfather Pelican," said Hideaway, ". . . by the way they always turn to me for food."

"You'll have to be," Storm Boy told him, "because their own father and mother are dead."

"Well, they needn't think I can spend all my time catching fish for them. Look at that fellow sitting up as if he owns the place."

"Oh, that's Mr Proud," said Storm Boy.

"How do you do, Mr Proud." Hideaway bowed and scratched the top of the pelican's head. "And what's your brother's name?"

"That's Mr Ponder," Storm Boy said. "He's very wise and serious."

"And what about the tiny fellow?" asked Hideaway. "Is he Mr Peep?"

"No, he's Mr Percival." Storm Boy picked up the bird gently in the scarf and held him on his lap. "He's been very sick."

"Welcome," said Hideaway. "And now Grandfather Pelican had better go and catch some fish or there won't be any tea for three Mr P's." And he went off down to his boat.

And that was how Mr Proud, Mr Ponder and Mr Percival came to live with Storm Boy.

Before long the three pelicans were big and strong. Their white necks curved up cleanly, their creels grew, and their upper beaks shone like pink pearlshell.

Every morning they spread their great white wings with the bold black edges and flew three or four times round the humpy and the beach near by to make sure that everything was in order for the new day. By then they thought it was time for breakfast, so they landed heavily beside the humpy, took a few dignified steps forward, and lined up at the back door. If Hideaway and Storm Boy were still in bed, the three birds stood politely for a little while waiting for some sign of movement or greeting. But if nothing happened after five or ten minutes, Mr Proud and Mr Ponder began to get impatient and started rattling their beaks in disapproval—a snippery-snappery, snickery-snackery sort of sound like dry reeds crackling—until someone woke up.

"All right! All right!" Storm Boy would say sleepily. "I can hear you, Mr Proud!"

He would sit up and look at the three gentlemen standing there on parade.

"I know what you're thinking, Mr Ponder. Time for respectable people to be up."

"Time for respectable pelicans to get their *own* breakfast," Hideaway grumbled, "instead of begging from their friends."

And as time went on, he really meant what he said.

At last Hideaway spoke sternly to Storm Boy.

"Mr Proud, Mr Ponder, and Mr Percival will have to go back to the sanctuary where they came from. We just can't afford to feed them any more."

Storm Boy was sad, but he always knew when his father had made up his mind. "Yes, Dad," he said.

"We'll put them in the big fish-baskets," said Hideaway, "and take them in the boat."

"Yes, Dad." Storm Boy hung his head.

So they caught Mr Proud first, and then Mr Ponder, held their wings against their sides, and put them firmly in the fish-baskets. Neither Mr Proud nor Mr Ponder thought much of the idea. They snackered noisily at Hideaway, raked their ruffled feathers crossly, and glared out through the wickerwork with their yellow eyes.

"Huh!" Hideaway laughed. "We've offended the two gentlemen. Never mind, it's all for their own good," and he bowed first to Mr Proud and then to Mr Ponder.

But when it came to Mr Percival's turn, Storm Boy couldn't bear to see him shut up too. Ever since the miracle of Mr Percival's rescue, he had been Storm Boy's favourite. He was always quieter, more gentle, and more trusting, than his two brothers. Storm Boy picked him up, smoothed his wings, and held him close. "Poor Mr. Percival," he said gently. He looked up at his father. "I'll hold Mr Percival," he said. "Can I, Dad?"

"Oh, all right," Hideaway said, taking up the two baskets. "Come on, it's time we started."

Hideaway sailed for five miles up the sanctuary before he stopped the boat.

"Here we are," he said at last.

Then he opened the two baskets and took out Mr Proud and Mr Ponder.

"Off you go," he said. "Now you'll have to look after yourselves." Then he pushed them off. They flew away in a high wide arc and made for the shore.

"Now Mr Percival," he said.

Storm Boy pressed his head against Mr Percival's and gave his friend a last soft squeeze. "Goodbye Mr Percival," he said. He had to pause for a second to clear his throat. "Be a . . . be a good pelican, Mr Percival, and look after yourself."

He lifted him over the side of the boat and put him down on the water as if he were a big rubber duck. Mr Percival looked surprised and pained for a minute and floated up and down on the ripples. Then he lifted his big wings, pedalled strongly, and rose slowly up over the water.

Storm Boy brushed at his eye with his knuckles and looked away. He didn't want to let his father see his face.

Hideaway and Storm Boy spent the day fishing. It was fine and sunny, but somehow it seemed cold. Most of the time they just sat in the bobbing boat without talking, but Storm Boy knew that his father knew what he was thinking. Sometimes Hideaway looked at him strangely, and once he even cleared his throat carefully, gazed out across the water, and said in an unhappy gay voice: "Well, I wonder how the three Mr P's are feeling. As happy as can be, I'll bet!" He looked rather miserably at Storm Boy and went on with his fishing.

"Yes, I'll bet," Storm Boy said, and also went on sadly with his fishing.

Towards evening they packed up and set off for home. The sun was flinging a million golden mirrors in a lane across the water. It glowed on the bare patches of the sandhills and lit up the bushes and tussocks till every stem and twig shone with rosy fire. The little boat came gliding in to shore through the chuckle of the ripples.

Suddenly Storm Boy looked up.

"Look, Dad! Look!" he shouted.

Hideaway beached the boat and looked up to where Storm Boy was pointing. "What?"

"Look! Look!" cried Storm Boy.

High against the sky on the big sandhill stood the tall lookout post that Hideaway and Fingerbone had put up years before. And right on top of the post was a big shape. It was quite still, a statue on a column, a bird of stone.

Then, as if hearing Storm Boy's startled voice, it suddenly spread out two big wings and launched itself into the air. As it banked against the western sun its beak and big black-tipped wings glowed in the shooting beams of light. For an instant it looked like a magic bird. Storm Boy ran ahead, craning upwards, yelling and waving.

"Mr Percival! It's Mr Percival! Mr Percival has come back home!"

It was a happy reunion that night. Even Hideaway seemed secretly glad that Mr Percival had come back.

"Yes, I suppose he can stay," he said; "as long as Mr Proud and Mr Ponder don't come back, too. One pelican's appetite is bad enough; we can't cope with three."

And although Storm Boy loved Mr Proud and Mr Ponder too, he found himself hoping very much that they would stay away.

And they did. As the days went by they sometimes swept overhead, or even landed on the beach for a while, but in the end they always returned to the sanctuary.

But not Mr Percival. He refused even to leave Storm Boy's side.

Wherever Storm Boy went, Mr Percival followed.

If he collected shells along the beach, Mr Percival went with him, either waddling importantly along at his heels or flying slowly above him in wide circles. If Storm Boy went swimming, or sliding down the sandhills, or playing on the sand, Mr Percival found a good spot near by and perched there heavily to watch and wait until it was over. If Storm Boy went fishing or rowing on the Coorong, Mr Percival cruised joyously round him with his neck bent back and his chest thrust forward like a dragon-ship sailing calmly in a sea of air. Whenever he saw Storm Boy anchor the boat he came gliding in with a long skimming splash, shook his wings into place, and bobbed serenely on the ripples a few yards away.

"Oh, you're a grand old gentleman, Mr Percival," Hideaway said, laughing. "You ought to be wearing a top-hat, or maybe a back-to-front collar and a pair of spectacles. Then perhaps you could give the sermon or take the Sunday school lessons."

But Mr Percival merely held his head on one side and waited for Hideaway to throw him a piece of fish—or two or three whole fish to pop into his creel.

Fingerbone and Hideaway were both glad that Storm Boy had found Mr Percival.

"Better than a watch-dog even," Fingerbone said. "Can't run much, but can *fly*."

"Can even chase after things like a dog," said Hideaway. "You watch!"

It was true. They first learnt what a good catcher Mr Percival was when Storm Boy was playing ball on the beach. It was a red and yellow ball that Hideaway had brought back from Goolwa. Once when Storm Boy threw it hard it went bouncing off toward Mr Percival.

"Look out!" Storm Boy shouted.

But Mr Percival didn't look out. Instead he took two or three quick steps and snapped up the ball in his creel. Storm Boy was horrified. He rushed up to Mr Percival, panting.

"You can't eat a *ball*," he yelled. "It's rubber, it's not a fish! Don't swallow it; you'll choke!"

Mr Percival listened to him very seriously for a minute, with his head held a bit more to one side than usual and his big beak parted in a sly smile. Then he stepped forward and dropped the ball at Storm Boy's feet, just like a retriever.

After that, Storm Boy often had fun on the beach with Mr Percival. Whenever he threw the ball, or a smooth pebble, or a sea-urchin, or an old fishing reel, Mr Percival snapped it up and brought it back. Sometimes he threw things into the water. Mr Percival watched carefully with his bright eyes; then he flew out, landed on the right spot, and fished the prize out of the water. Then Storm Boy would laugh and clap his hands and rub his fingers up and down the back of Mr Percival's neck. Mr Percival always liked this very much; the only thing he liked better was a good meal of fish.

One day as Hideaway was watching them play he had an idea.

"If he can bring things back to you, perhaps he can carry things away too," he said. He gave Mr Percival a sinker and a bit of fishing line. "Now, take it to Storm Boy," he said; "that's the fellow."

At times Mr Percival didn't understand, but at last, after many tries, he dropped the sinker at Storm Boy's feet. Both Hideaway and Storm Boy clapped, and rubbed the back of Mr Percival's neck, and gave him a piece of fish. Mr Percival looked very pleased and proud.

After that Hideaway asked Storm Boy to stand out in the shallow water, and they played the game again. Before long Mr Percival could take a sinker and a small fishing line, fly out to Storm Boy, and drop it beside him. But he always expected a piece of fish after each try.

They played the game for many weeks, sometimes with Storm Boy in the water and sometimes with Hideaway, until Mr Percival could carry a fishing line and drop it into the sea without any trouble. Then, when there was an off-shore wind from the north and the great seas flattened out sullenly, Hideaway went far out from shore and Mr Percival practised carrying a long, long line to him.

"It's wonderful," Hideaway said, laughing and clapping when he came back. "Now Mr Percival can help me with my fishing. He can carry out my mulloway lines for me." And he scratched Mr Percival's neck and gave him an extra piece of fish. "Mr Percival, you're as clever as a Chinese fishing bird," he said. And then he laughed, and so did Storm Boy; and Mr Percival was so pleased with himself that he snickered and snackered happily for the rest of the day.

As time went by people began to talk about Storm Boy and Mr Percival. Picknickers and Game Inspectors and passing fishermen saw them and began to spread the story.

"Follows him round like a dog," said old Sammy Scales in Goolwa. "Crazy, I tell you."

"I wouldn't have believed it," the postmaster said, "if I hadn't seen it with my own eyes."

And not long after that many people did see it with their own eyes. For when Hideaway and Storm Boy set off on their trips to Goolwa, Mr Percival couldn't understand what was happening. He flew around and behind and ahead of them all the way, until they began to get near the town; then he landed and waited patiently on the river, until he saw the boat starting off for home again.

People used to hear about it and come to watch. "Just like a dog," said Sammy Scales. "Crazy, I tell you. Some day the whole world will hear about this."

And then something happened that proved he was right.

It was the year of the great storms. They began in May, even before the winter had started. Shrieking and raging out of the south the Antarctic winds seemed to have lost themselves and come up howling in a frenzy to find the way. In June they flattened the sedge, rooted out some of the bushes that had crouched on top of the sandhills for years, and blew out one of the iron sheets from the humpy. Hideaway tied wires to the walls and weighed down the roof with driftwood and stones.

In July the winds lost their senses. Three great storms swept out of the south, the third one so terrible that it gathered up the sea in mountains, mashed it into foam, and hurled it against the shore. The waves came in like rolling railway embankments right up to the sandhills where Hideaway and Storm Boy lived. They lashed and tore at them as if they wanted to carry them away. The boobyalla bushes bent and broke. The humpy shivered and shook. Even Mr Percival had to go right inside or risk being blown away.

As night came on, Hideaway battened up the doorway and spread extra clothing on the bunks.

"Better sleep now if you can," he said to Storm Boy. "By morning the humpy might be blowing along on the other side of the Coorong."

In the darkness of early morning Storm Boy suddenly woke with Hideaway's voice in his ears.

"Quick, Storm Boy," he said.

Storm Boy jumped up. "Is the humpy blowing away?"

"No, it's a wreck!" Hideaway said. "A shipwreck on the shore."

Storm Boy put on two of his father's coats and followed him out to the top of the sandhill. Daybreak was coming like a milky stain in the east, but the world in front was just a white roar. Hideaway put his mouth close to Storm Boy's ear and pointed.

"Look!" he yelled. "Out there!"

Storm Boy looked hard. There was a black shape in the white. Fingerbone was standing on top of the sandhill holding on to the lookout post.

"Tugboat," he shouted.

"Aground!" yelled Hideaway.

Fingerbone nodded. "Storm too wild," he bellowed. "Poor fellows on tugboat. . . ." He shook his head. "Poor fellows!"

When at last morning came over the world they could see the tugboat clearly, lying like a wounded whale, with huge waves leaping and crashing over it, throwing up white hands of spray in a devil-dance.

"They can never swim it or launch a boat," said Hideaway. "Their only hope is a line to the shore."

"No one get line out," Fingerbone said. "Not today."

"No," said Hideaway sadly. "And by tomorrow it

will be too late." Sometimes in a lull between the waves they could see three or four men clinging to the tug-boat, waving their hands for help.

"Look at them," Storm Boy yelled. "We must help them! They'll be drowned."

"How can we help?" asked his father. "We can't throw a line; it's too far."

"How far is it?"

"Too far. Two or three hundred yards at least."

"No blackfellow throw spear so far," said Finger-bone. "Not even half so far."

"Especially not with a line attached. We'd need a harpoon gun."

"Then I couldn't throw a stone a *quarter* of the way," Storm Boy said. He picked up a pebble and hurled it towards the sea. It fell near the shore. "See," he said.

Suddenly there was a swish of big wings past them and Mr Percival sailed out over the spot where the pebble had fallen. He looked at the foam of the waves for a minute as if playing the old game of fetch-the-pebble-back; then he changed his mind, turned, and landed back on the beach.

Storm Boy gave a great shout and ran towards him. "Mr Percival! Mr Percival is the one to do it! He can *fly!*"

Hideaway saw what he meant. He raced back to the humpy and found two or three long fishing lines, as thin as thread. He tied them together and coiled them very carefully and lightly on a hard patch of clean sand. Then he took a light sinker, tied it to one end, and gave it to Mr. Percival.

"Out to the ship," he said, pointing and flapping; "take it out to the ship."

Mr Percival looked puzzled and alarmed at the idea of fishing on such a wild day, but he beat his wings and rose up heavily over the sea.

"Out to the boat! Out to the boat!" they all shouted. But Mr Percival didn't understand. He flew too far to one side, dropped the line in the sea, and turned back.

"Missed," said Hideaway, disappointed.

"But it was a good try," Storm Boy said, as Mr Percival landed. He gave him a piece of fish and scratched his neck. "Good boy," he said. "Good boy, Mr Percival. In a minute we'll have another try."

But they missed again. This time Mr Percival flew straight towards the boat but didn't go out quite far enough. "Never mind," said Storm Boy. "You're a good pelican for trying." He held Mr Percival in his arms and gave him another piece of fish.

Again and again they tried, and again and again they missed. At first the men on the boat couldn't understand what was going on, but they soon guessed, and watched every try hopefully and breathlessly.

Storm Boy and Hideaway were disappointed but they didn't give up. Neither did Mr Percival. He flew out and back, out and back, until at last, on the tenth try, he did it. A great gust of wind suddenly lifted him up and flung him sideways. He threw up his big wing and, just as he banked sharply over the tug-boat, dropped the line. It fell right across the drowning ship.

"You've done it! You've done it!" Storm Boy, Hideaway, and Fingerbone shouted together as Mr Percival landed on the beach. "You're a good, brave, clever pelican." And they patted him, and fed him, and danced round him so much that poor Mr Percival couldn't quite understand what he'd done that was so wonderful. He kept snickering and snackering excitedly, opening his beak in a kind of grin, and eating more fish than he'd ever had before.

But the struggle to save the men on the tugboat was only just beginning. The captain seized the fishing line as it fell, waited for the next big wave to roll past, and then fastened the line to the end of a long coil of thin rope. Gently, very gently, he lowered it into the sea and waved to Hideaway and Fingerbone to start pulling. They had to be very careful; if the line snagged, or if they pulled too sharply, the line might break and they would have to start all over again.

But they were lucky. At last the rope came lifting and flopping slowly out of the backwash. Fingerbone ran down to grab it. He danced and waved excitedly. Now the captain of the tug tied a heavy line to the thin rope, and the crew kept paying them out together, holding on desperately as the big waves and spray smashed over their ship.

Before long, Storm Boy, Fingerbone, and Hideaway had hauled the end of the big rope ashore. Then they dragged it quickly up the sandhills to the lookout post, where Hideaway wound it firmly round and round the butt. Meanwhile the crew had fastened their end and had hitched a rough kind of bosun's chair to the rope. A man lashed himself in, and signalled to Hideaway to start pulling on the thin rope. The rescue was ready to start.

The sea sprang and snatched at the man on the rope like a beast with white teeth. Sometimes, where the rope sagged lowest, the waves swept him right under. Storm Boy could feel the shock and shudder of the line as the water thundered round it. But the man managed to snatch a breath between waves and he always rose up safely again on the rope. Hideaway and Fingerbone pulled until their feet dug deep into the sand, and the muscles that stood out on their arms looked like the rope they were pulling. And so at last they were able to haul the man through the thud and tug of the sea to the shore, where he unfastened himself and dropped down on the sand. He was shivering and exhausted, but he was safe. Storm Boy ran down to help him up to the humpy.

Meanwhile the rest of the crew had hauled the rough bosun's chair back to the ship and another man was ready to be pulled ashore. After him came a third, who staggered feebly up the beach.

"Hurry," he said. "The boat's breaking up and there are still three men on board."

Hideaway's forehead was wet, and Fingerbone puffed as they dug their feet in the sand and hauled.

"Hurry," they kept panting. "The boat's breaking up."

At last they had five men safely on shore and there was only the captain to come. Then he, too, left the ship and they hauled again. He was a big man who weighed down the rope, and Hideaway and Fingerbone were almost exhausted. Suddenly the rope grew taut, shuddered, and slackened.

"Quick," Hideaway cried. "She's shifting."

Storm Boy seized the pulling-rope and hauled. "Hurry," yelled the captain. "She's going."

One or two of the crewmen who could still walk grabbed the line and helped to pull. Between them all they slowly hauled the captain ashore and dragged him, pale and half drowned on to the beach.

"Saved!" he kept saying weakly. "Saved by a miracle and a pelican."

Hideaway and Storm Boy kept the captain and his five crewmen in the humpy for a day. They gave them hot food and dried out their clothes. Next morning the storm started to clear and the sun flashed across the Coorong, so Hideaway began preparing to sail the six of them up to Goolwa.

Before they left, the captain took Hideaway aside.

"You saved our lives," he said, "you and your black friend, and especially the boy and the bird. We want to do something in return."

Hideaway was embarrassed. "No need to worry about that," he said.

"But we've talked it over," said the captain, "and we've decided. We'd like to pay for the boy to go to school—to boarding school in Adelaide."

Hideaway was sad. "He'd be very lonely, and so would I. His heart would be sick for the wind and the waves, and especially for Mr Percival."

"No matter," the captain said. "He's ten, or is it eleven? Soon he'll be grown up, and yet he won't be able to read or write. It's not right to stop him."

Hideaway hung his head. "Yes, you're right, he ought to go."

But when they called Storm Boy and told him the captain's plan, he wouldn't go. "No!" he said horrified. "I won't leave Mr Percival! I won't! Not unless I'm allowed to take Mr Percival to school with me."

"You know you couldn't do that!"

"Then I won't go."

The captain shrugged. "Very well," he said to Hideaway. "Later perhaps. There'll always be a place ready for him." Then he said goodbye and scratched Mr

Percival's neck. "You're a big, wonderful bird," he said. He looked up at Hideaway. "When he dies you must send him to the museum; we'll put a label on the case: *The pelican that saved six men's lives.*"

Hideaway looked round quickly. He was glad Storm Boy hadn't heard the captain's words.

For the rest of the year everyone was happy. The storms went back to the cold south, the sun warmed the sandhills, and spring ran over the countryside with new leaves and little bush buds.

Before long the open season for duck-shooting came round again. All along the Coorong the shooters went, the blast of their guns echoing up and down the water, and the stench of their gunpowder hanging on the still air like a black fog of rotting smoke. The mornings were filled with the cries and screams of birds. Sometimes Storm Boy could see the birds falling, or struggling westward, wounded and maimed, towards the shelter of the sanctuary.

From the start, Mr Percival hated the shooters. He harried them whenever he could. Sometimes he just sat staring at them rudely until they grew impatient and chased him away. Sometimes he swam annoyingly near their hidden boats until they splashed or made a noise. But most of all he flew round and round their hiding places in wide circles like a cumbersome old aeroplane on patrol. And all of it was to help the ducks, to warn them in time, to keep them away from the shooters, so that the terrible guns would roar less often, and kill less often.

Before long the ducks understood Mr Percival's warnings, and kept away. The shooters grew angrier and angrier.

"It's that confounded, pot-bellied old pelican again," they'd say. "He's worse than a seal in a fish-net."

"He's like a spy in the sky," said one. "We'll never shoot any ducks while he's about."

And so it went on until one terrible morning in February. Storm Boy was standing high on the ridge of a sandhill watching the sun slip up from the sea like a blazing penny. He turned to look inland, and there behind a bending boobyalla bush near the Coorong he saw two shooters crouching. They were very still, waiting for six ducks out on the water to swim a little nearer. Just then Mr Percival came sweeping by in his ponderous flight. He swung in low over the hiding men, and the ducks gave a sudden cry of alarm, flapped strongly, and flew off very fast and low over the water.

The men shouted with rage. One of them leapt out, swung up his gun, and aimed at Mr Percival. Storm Boy saw him and gave a great cry.

"Don't shoot! Don't shoot! It's Mr Perc . . ."

His voice was drowned by the roar of the gun. Mr Percival seemed to shudder in flight as if he'd flown into a wall of glass. Then he started to fall heavily and awkwardly to the ground. Storm Boy ran headlong towards the spot, tripping, falling over tussocks, stumbling into hollows, jumping up, racing, panting, crying out, gulping in big sobs, his heart pumping wildly.

"Mr Percival! They've shot Mr Percival!" he kept screaming. "Mr Percival! Mr Percival!"

Poor Mr Percival! When Storm Boy reached him he was trying to stand up and walk, but he fell forwards helplessly with one wing splayed out. Blood was moistening his white chest-feathers, and he was panting as if he'd just played a hard game.

"Mr Percival! Oh, Mr Percival!" It was all Storm Boy could say. He kept on repeating it over and over again as he picked him up slowly and gently and then ran all the way back to the humpy.

Hideaway was getting the breakfast when Storm Boy burst in, sobbing.

"Mr Percival! They've shot Mr Percival!"

Hideaway sprang round, startled, threw down the spoon he was using, and ran out to find the shooters. But they'd already gone. Ashamed and afraid, they'd quickly crossed to the other side of the Coorong, and driven off.

Hideaway came back angrily. Then he took Mr Percival gently from Storm Boy and examined him— wiped his chest and straightened the shattered feathers of his wing. Mr Percival snackered his beak weakly and panted rapidly.

"Will he . . . will Mr Percival . . . be all right?" Storm Boy could hardly get the words out.

Hideaway handed the wounded bird back to him silently and looked out through the doorway towards the far track where the shooters had disappeared. He couldn't bring himself to say anything.

All day long Storm Boy held Mr Percival in his arms. In front of the rough iron stove where long ago he had first nursed the little bruised pelican into life, he now sat motionless and silent. Fingerbone tried to cheer him up, and Hideaway offered him breakfast and dinner, but Storm Boy shook his head and sat on, numb and silent. Now and then he smoothed the feathers where they were matted and stuck together, or straightened the useless wing. But in his heart he knew what was happening. Mr Percival's breathing was shallow and quick, his body and neck were drooping, and for long stretches at a time his eyes were shut. Then, suddenly, they would snap open again, clear and bright, and he would snacker his beak softly in a kind of sad, weak smile, before dozing off again.

"Mr Percival," Storm Boy whispered, "you're the best, best friend I ever had."

Tea-time came, the sun dipped down, and long shadows began to move up from the hollows. For a while the tops of the high sandhills glowed golden in the evening light, but then they faded too and it was dark. Hideaway didn't light the lantern. Instead, the three of them stayed on in front of the little fireplace—Hideaway, Storm Boy, and Mr Percival—while darkness filled the humpy and the stars came out as clear and pure as ice.

And at nine o'clock Mr Percival died.

Only then did Hideaway move. He got up softly, and, gently, very gently, took Mr Percival from Storm Boy. And Storm Boy gave him up. Then at last he flung himself down on his bunk and sobbed softly to himself, hour after hour, until Hideaway came over and put a hand on his shoulder.

"It's right that you should cry for Mr Percival for a while," he said, kindly and firmly; "but don't keep on brooding, Storm Boy."

"B—But why did they shoot Mr . . . Mr Percival? He wasn—wasn't hurting anyone; just—just warning the ducks like always."

"In the world," Hideaway said sadly, "there will always be men who are cruel, just as there will always be men who are lazy or stupid or wise or kind. Today you've seen what cruel and stupid men can do."

He pulled a blanket over Storm Boy and said quietly, "Now try to get some sleep."

But Storm Boy didn't sleep. All night he lay clutching his cold wet pillow.

In the morning Hideaway spoke to Storm Boy.

"The sailors will arrange to have Mr Percival put in the museum," he said, "with a notice saying that he saved their lives—and telling how he lost his. Would you like that?"

Storm Boy shook his head. "Mr Percival wouldn't have liked that," he said; "not to be shut up in a glass case for people to stare at. Never!"

And he took the spade and climbed to the top of the big sandhill by the lookout post.

"Mr Percival would want to be buried here," he said, "by the foot of the lookout. This is his place for ever." And he began to dig.

Hideaway nodded. Then he took a shovel and went up to dig too.

And so they buried Mr Percival deep beside the lookout post on top of the golden sandhill, with the beach below, and the shining sand and the salt smack of the sea there day and night—and all around was the wide sky, and the tang of the open air, and the wild lonely wind in the scrub.

When they'd finished, Storm Boy stood for a long time looking silently all around him. Then he turned to Hideaway.

"All right," he said, "I'm ready to go now if you like."

"Go? Where to?"

"To school! Like the sailors said."

"Oh Oh, yes. . . . Very well, then."

Hideaway knew then that without Mr Percival Storm Boy wouldn't be able to live there; at least not for a while.

Together they walked slowly down the sandhill to the humpy.

"We'll leave the boat in Goolwa for a few days," Hideaway said. "I'll have to go up to Adelaide with you to get you settled in."

And that was how Storm Boy went to school. Hideaway came back to the humpy by the Coorong to start the long, long wait for the school holidays. By day, Fingerbone sometimes comes to talk to him, but at night he stands alone beside the lookout post and gazes out at the sea and the clouds of the western storms; and, a hundred miles away in Adelaide, Storm Boy sits by the boarding school window and looks out at the tossing trees and the windy sky.

And everything lives on in their hearts—the wind-talk and wave-talk, and the scribblings on the sand; the Coorong, the salt smell of the beach, the humpy, and the long days of their happiness together. And always, above them, in their mind's eye, they can see the shape of two big wings in the storm-clouds and the flying scud—two wings of white with trailing black edges—spread across the sky.

For birds like Mr Percival do not really die.

The Lock-Out

As soon as Jim woke up he knew that the week-end was going to be different. For one thing his parents were flying to Melbourne to attend some conference or other, and old Gran was coming to sit in. That gave the place a different flavour for a start; it was like looking ahead to a scout camp or a barbecue in the bush. Then there was the grand final of the metropolitan high schools football association on Saturday morning, and he, Jim Bear, was one of the hopes of Hamilton High. Of course Gran would have added that today was Friday the Thirteenth—a date to daunt all living creatures except lions and lunatics—but Jim laughed at that. Superstition was meant for old wives and grandmothers.

He got up and had a long, hot shower, sousing and splashing like a water buffalo. *Hamilton High, Hamilton High*, he yelled, composing one of the twenty Bear variations of his team's war cry.

"Look at the look of a hot shot guy,
Take a look at his look, then lie down and die."

"Ow!" he interposed as the water suddenly steamed and boiled; "turn off that cold tap wherever you are." The temperature slowly righted itself.

"You'll be dead,
You'll be bled,
You'll be spread, spread, s-p-r-e-a-d,
All over the oval by Hamilton High."

He was still finishing his breakfast when the cab called to take his mother and father to the airport. His mother fussed and farewelled.

"Now, remember to feed the cat, Jim dear," she repeated breathlessly. "Oh, and don't forget to tell Gran that the pot-roast is in the oven. She'll be down this afternoon."

"Yes, Mum."

"And remember to put out the milk bottles before you go to bed."

"Yes, Mum."

"And lock the doors. We can't be too careful with that dreadful peeping-tom still prowling about."

"Yes, Mum."

"We'll be back on Sunday afternoon's plane. Have you copied down our Melbourne address?"

"Yes, Mum."

"And the telephone number?"

"Yes, Mum."

"Good luck for your match tomorrow."

"Thanks, Mum."

"And behave yourself. Don't go anywhere without telling Gran."

"No, Mum."

"Goodbye, Jim dear."

"Goodbye, Mum."

When the cab had gone he stacked the dishes in the sink and collected his school books. He was about to slam the front door when he remembered that the latchkey his mother had given him was still lying on the dresser in his room. "Have to be a bit smarter than that, Jim boy," he said to himself as he strode back to get it. "Lock yourself out of your own house if you're not careful. Be a nice way to start the week-end." He swung his long leg over the seat of his bicycle, pushed his bag between the handlebars, and rode off, whistling *Hamilton High*.

Behind him the house at No. 6 Valencia Grove waited, silent and empty. Like all the other houses in its street it stood decently back in its garden, sheltered by trees and an apron of Mrs Bear's favourite espaliered roses. All round it there were more houses with fences and roses, and more streets, kerbs, and footpaths that spread out in joints and rectangles from suburb to suburb into a vast jigsaw of bitumen and cement and tiles that ran for thirty miles from Port Noarlunga to Elizabeth. It was Jim Bear's world.

The road up to Hamilton High School undulated for a mile or so along the southern foothills, and the power lines leap-frogged from pole to pole by its side. Jim slowly ground his way past them.

"G'day, Herc!"

"Hi, Boomer!"

It was his team mate, Boomer Ryan, centre half forward in the big game tomorrow, with a face like an ironbark and a voice like a thunderstorm. He was paying Jim the compliment of his nickname—Hercules. Not that Jim was a giant, but he was big for a fellow of fifteen, with well-built shoulders and thighs.

"Feelin' fit?"

"Okay I guess."

"Better be."

"Enough to wipe off East Adelaide."

"Reckon."

They swung off their bikes and walked the last hundred yards, pushing and leaning forward like old men in a storm. Boomer panted out his thoughts between gasps:

"Won't hardly be able to sleep tonight. . . . Premiership and all."

"C'n say that again."

"You sleep all right, can you, Herc?"

"Not before a big match."

"Better do tonight."

"I'm on my own tonight. Just me and Gran."

"No kiddin'?"

"Yeah."

"With old Gran Williams—the one that's always wheezin' with asthma or somethin'?"

"Yeah. Dad and Mum're in Melbourne."

"How's about that! They'll miss the match." Boomer's voice rose accusingly.

"Had to, Dad reckoned. Some crummy conference in Melbourne."

"No conference is important enough to miss the match."

" 's what I reckon."

"A lot will, though. Our own kids even."

"Yeah."

"No idea what's the right thing."

"No."

"Teachers even. Old Parrotnose, can you see him comin'?"

"Not likely."

"No."

"No."

"Or the boss?"

But Boomer was quick to defend the headmaster's taste for football. "Yes, he'll be there. Too right he will. But not Parrotnose. He wouldn't know a ball from a bull's foot."

Parrotnose was the figurative but none the less appropriate name the boys used for their class teacher, Mr Gabriel Hecht—a fine scientist but hardly a football addict. Jim and Boomer pushed their bikes into the rack and sauntered over to the quadrangle.

"You know what?" Boomer asked suddenly.

"No, what?"

"Today's Friday the Thirteenth."

"Yeah."

"Just as well it's not tomorrow."

"You don't believe in that stuff, do you?"

"Not half! It's a helluva day for things to happen to you."

"Yuk!"

"Be nice if you broke a leg or somethin'—the big match and all comin' up tomorrow"

"Just superstition."

"Yeah? I'd sooner be on the safe side all the same; no sense in rubbin' superstition up the wrong way."

Jim laughed. But then, he didn't know what was going to happen to him that day.

The first disaster occurred at the end of Mr Hecht's science lesson. The class was running late, and Mr Hecht was haranguing them about speed and punctuality. "Hurry up, Carter," he shouted. "Flasks in the cupboard, test tubes in the rack. Hampel, wipe up that mess by the sink." He looked at it more closely. "What is it, for heaven's sake? Chocolate fudge? I must ask Miss Hendry to reserve you a place in the Home Science class." Rodney Rudnick tittered ingratiatingly, but Mr Hecht flashed at him: "Don't stand there tittering, Rudnick, you big boob. Put those tripods away. Anderson, the beakers on the shelf. Heaslip, the stools. Bear, carry that Winchester quart into the store-room."

Mr Hecht should have remembered that it was Friday the Thirteenth, but he didn't. And so Jim walked straight into the store-room and there came face to face with fate and superstition, all at once. For there wasn't any room for the Winchester jar. Rows and rows of chemicals stood side by side—stoppered bottles, flasks with labels, coloured fluids, and crystals, a mixture of things pungent and putrid and aromatic. But no space for the jar. "Hurry up, Bear," Mr Hecht called. "What are you doing in there—drinking the stuff?" There was one small space on the second shelf. Jim hoisted up the jar and jostled it in, forcing the other flasks and bottles gently to each side. It was a silly thing to do, especially on such a day. A jar of concentrated silver nitrate solution tilted suddenly to the right, teetered for a second, and then poured a terrible Niagara down on to the bench below. There it splashed and leapt in a thousand directions just as Jim, with an agonized lunge, tried to save the jar. His face momentarily dipped to the level of the bench and the spray spattered his cheeks and chin, his forehead and nose, the lobes of his ears and the whole white plane of his shirt front with its deadly rain. In an instant he was pock-marked with black freckles, tattooed, black-leaded, daubed with spots until he looked like a rejected painting from an off-beat studio.

Luckily none of the drops struck his eyes. His yell of anguish and disbelief filled the store-room and stung Mr Hecht next door. He leapt forward just as Jim emerged, brushing futilely at the mess on his clothes and hands.

"Bear!"

"Sorry, sir!"

"Are you all right?"

"Yes, sir. Yes, I'm all right."

"What in God's name have you done?"

"Tipped over the silver nitrate solution, sir. Least, that's what I hope it is."

"You *hope* it is?"

"I mean, I hope it's nothing worse, sir."

"Nothing worse! You'll be black for a month, boy. Quick, get it off, get it off. You look like a chimney sweep."

But it was too late. Despite Mr Hecht's genuine haste and concern, the best that Jim could achieve, apart from a damaged coat and a ruined shirt, was a kind of variegated skin texture that made him look like a Hottentot with smallpox. After having been scrubbed and rubbed three times at school, paraded before the headmaster and taken to the doctor, he was sent home for the rest of the day. Jim didn't know whether this was out of consideration for his health, or because nobody at school could bear to look at him.

He made himself some noodle soup from a packet in the cupboard, ate four pieces of bread and jam, and half emptied the gallon of ice-cream in the refrigerator. Then he inspected his face in the mirror again, rubbed it with sandsoap and detergent until the pink patches glowed delicately like shells between the charcoal smudges, and finally went to his own room and lay down on his bed. It seemed the safest way of dealing with the rest of Friday the Thirteenth. Under the warmth of the rug and the drowsy hum of the afternoon outside, he slowly fell asleep.

Gran arrived by cab at three o'clock. She let herself in with the latchkey her daughter had given her, and bustled about with her things in the hall. Then she carried her coat and hat to the spare room at the end of the passage. On the way back she glanced in at

Jim's door—and had the first of her bad turns. Unexpectedly there was a body in the bed. She clasped her chest and waddled uncertainly up to it. "Jim!" she exclaimed, aghast. The sleeper gave a half snore and exposed his face. Gran started and had her second bad turn.

"Smallpox," she wheezed, catching her breath. "Dear God, the boy is down with the smallpox!" And with her hands alternately clasping her cheeks and her chest she ran a grandmotherly run to the phone and breathlessly called the doctor. The nurse on duty gathered from the incoherent gabbling that, whatever was happening at No. 6 Valencia Grove, it was a matter of life or death. As Gran hung up she was seized with a violent attack of asthma and sat hunched up in a lounge room chair, blue in the face and choking for breath.

Jim woke up with a start. "Gran!" he said to himself. "That's Gran!" He ran into the lounge. "Gran, are you all right?" Gran looked up momentarily, saw the sooty and pock-marked face above her, and cringed away hysterically. "The doctor! The doctor! He's coming."

"Right!" Jim said. "Just hang on, Gran. He'll fix you up." Gran looked at him uncomprehendingly. "Bed," she said weakly. "You poor boy."

Jim had forgotten about his face. He was filled with concern for the old woman's health, and with admiration for her presence of mind.

"Quick thinking, Gran," he said, "to call the doc like that."

She was seized with another bout and could only roll her eyes at him and wheeze inarticulately. He tried to help her. "Tablets?" he said.

"Tab . . . tablets?"

"Have you got any tablets?"

"No tab . . . tablets."

"Well, let me put you to bed."

A car braked suddenly outside, and footsteps sounded on the path.

"It's the doctor!" Jim ran to the door. "It's Gran, doctor. Asthma attack. Pretty bad, I think."

"Nurse said it sounded urgent." Dr Hobbs looked sideways at Jim as they strode down the hall. "What the devil have you done to your face?"

"Oh, that? Spilt a flask of silver nitrate solution. Splattered all over the place."

"Looks like it. Lucky it didn't get into your eyes."

They entered the lounge room, and the doctor bent over Gran. "Now, Mrs Williams, what's all this?" But he didn't spend long in examining her. "I think we'd better get her to hospital, Jim. Can I use your phone?"

"Sure, doctor. It's in here."

Poor Gran hardly had time to wheeze out a word. Within a few minutes an ambulance had carried her off and Jim was left standing on the front veranda watching it disappear up the street. It was only then that he realized his own situation. He was alone now, with a face like a minstrel's, and nobody to share the house with him for forty-eight hours.

By eleven o'clock that night Jim realized how slowly time went when you were on your own. Boomer called in for a while before tea to make sure Jim would be fit for the big match in the morning, but apart from that he spent the evening alone. He washed the dishes, fed the cat, watched TV, polished his boots, put out the milk bottles, locked the door, and sauntered about restlessly from room to room. It was a shock to see how dark and empty the house could be. Then, at the last minute, he remembered that his football shorts hadn't been washed after Thursday's practice, so he hastily doused them in detergent and warm water, rubbed the slide marks and dirty patches from the seat, and then drew them out looking over-scrubbed and bleached. After rinsing them and squeezing them as dry as he could he carried them up to the lounge room, turned on the gas fire, and hung the shorts over a chair to dry. He would have to iron them in the morning before the match. Ginger, the big tortoise-shell cat, flopped down in front of the fire with her engine going and her tail swishing in gentle ecstasy. For a while they tested each other's company with silent relish, watching the steam rising from the drying **shorts**.

The warm moisture gave Jim an idea—a hot bath. He looked at his watch. It was late, almost midnight, but he would sleep all the better for it. And so, by the time he had filled the bath, wallowed in it like a grampus, soaped himself three times, tested the way his legs suddenly grew heavier when he lifted them out of the water, measured the length of the hair on his shins, trimmed his toenails with his mother's nail scissors, and finally dried himself vigorously, it was past midnight.

But if he thought that Friday the Thirteenth had finished with him now, he was very much mistaken. The worst disaster of all was about to happen. He was standing on the bathmat, trying to dry the small of his back by rubbing it against the towel like an itchy horse against a tree, when he heard Ginger coughing. She had run out of the lounge room and now stood urgently at the front door, waiting to be let out, retching and hacking like a consumptive chain-smoker.

"Oh, my gosh!" Jim thought. "Fur-balling or biliousness." He suddenly remembered his mother's ominous warning: "If the cat wants to go outside, for heaven's sake don't keep it waiting." He leapt to the front door, swung it back, and held open the wrought-iron screen. But with a strangely feminine perversity the cat only ran forward a foot or two before crouching and convulsing again.

"Not there! Shoo! Ahh, for Pete's sake!" Jim hastily tied the towel round his waist, flicked off the light switch to avoid being exposed to public view, and swept her up in his hands.

"Out you go, whether you like it or not!" He ran across the veranda in his bare feet and tossed her gently on to the garden.

"Off you go! Shoo!"

As he turned to slip back inside again the breeze stirred; the hibiscus swayed by the steps, and the shadows moved in the street lights. Then gently, very gently, the front door swung shut and the latch sprang into the lock with a soft click. Horrified, Jim ran to the door, pushing and heaving. But he was too late. He was locked out. Locked out of his own house, at midnight, and without any clothes on.

For a second or two he cowered, appalled, in the corner of the veranda. But what had seemed so dim and secluded at first soon became more and more exposed as his eyes grew accustomed to the dark. Luckily there was nobody about. The street was deserted, the neighbours were all in bed. Although Jim's mind was still strangely numb, one thought charged about in it like a bull in a yard. He had to get back inside—this instant, before anyone saw him.

His only hope was an unlatched window. He skirted the hibiscus bush in the corner of the garden and made for the dining room. It looked out over the front lawn and held a long view up the curve of the street, but at least there was an off chance that the window there might be unlocked. As he stepped on to the soft grass of the lawn he was astonished to find himself walking on tip-toe. For a second he was vaguely aware of his own tension, a kind of catching himself by surprise before he plunged off across the grass.

For the first three strides the spring of the lawn under his feet was urgently pleasant, but at the fourth step he trod sharply on the garden hose not a foot from the end near the sprinkler, and a squirt of icy water shot out like an electric shock. He leapt up with a noisy gasp and ran to the window. But it was locked. He groaned at the thoroughness of his mother's anti-tom precautions and stood indecisively for a second, cold drops and runnels of water pausing and chasing down his calves.

Suddenly a car swung into the street and came bearing down on the house, its headlamps boring at him like searchlights. Too late Jim realized that he was being floodlit like a marble statue in the park, and he flung himself down, commando-style, on the lawn. The car took the curve at speed, and its slashing blade of light swung over him like a scimitar. Jim rose uncertainly to his feet, the soft prickle of the lawn stippling his chest and belly. It was a curiously cold, grassy feeling, but it seemed to salve the hot flush of his embarrassment and shame.

He ran for the other windows along the front of the house, testing each one in turn. They were all locked. Twice more a car raked the house with its headlights, and twice more Jim had to take violent evasive action. The second time, in flinging himself down recklessly behind the espaliered roses, he landed on some old cuttings that his mother had left lying there after her pruning. He only just resisted the impulse to yell and leap up, rolling over on his side in silent agony instead, his fingers trying to seal the cat's-claw scratches down his ribs. The girl in the car turned to her companion inquiringly:

"Darling, what was that thing in the garden there?"

"Dunno. Dog, I s'pose."

"But it looked sort of long and white. Like a pig."

"Ah-h, use your sense, Rosie. How could a white pig be running round the suburbs at this time of night?"

By the time Jim had probed the front and side of the house he was sore and exhausted. But fear drove him on. His only hope now lay in the windows at the back—in the kitchen, laundry, and toilet. But these looked down the steeply sloping backyard where the ground fell away. They were a foot or more beyond his reach. He looked round for a box or stool, but of course his mother was much too careful to have anything like that lying about the place. Despair began to numb his mind again, just as the creeping goose-pimples on his skin seemed to tighten and contract his body. And then, in a sort of despairing mental lunge, he thought of Mr Hogan's stepladder.

Ben Hogan next door was a good-natured little man who often lent things to the Bears. Jim himself had sometimes borrowed the stepladder from the old shed behind the tank. But there was the problem of getting it out and carrying it back. He couldn't possibly go round by the front gate, without clothes, at this time of night. It would have to be over the back fence—wooden palings five feet high, unpainted and needled all over with inch-long splinters. But a desperate plight called for desperate action.

Happily the two timber cross-pieces that held up the palings were on Jim's side, and he was able to get a foothold on them and swing a leg over the top. Then, with a sudden heave, he hoisted himself up, skinning his calves and thighs, until he was balanced unstably on top. He tied the towel more firmly round his waist and leapt—a kind of dismounting, bucking movement that deposited him on Mrs Hogan's pea-beans with a thud. He quickly disentangled himself and crept over to the woodshed.

For a while it looked as if his luck had changed. The ladder was there right enough, and he managed to half drag, half carry it across to the fence. This time it was going to be a lot easier; he could use the ladder to help himself over.

He stood the steps against the palings and climbed to the top; but here he struck unforeseen trouble, for how was he going to balance himself up there while he transferred the ladder from one side of the fence to the other? He tried squatting down on the paling-tops with one leg on each side, using the cross-bar as a brace for his left foot, but he couldn't get enough leverage that way, and in any case if his foot slipped he had a fair chance of bisecting himself.

He pondered the Archimedean problem, crouched there, riding the fence like a jockey. There was only one thing for it: he would have to stand up to get the extra purchase, and pull the ladder over in see-saw fashion. He jiggled himself along for a foot or two until he reached one of the square jarrah posts that held up the fence. There he managed to get himself shakily erect while he slowly turned round for the ladder. But the constant twisting and shuffling was too much for the towel round his middle. As he stood up and heaved, the single knot slipped open suddenly and the towel fell swiftly and silently down into Hogan's yard. And at that moment Mrs Hogan, no less fearful of peeping-toms than Jim's mother, and convinced that she could hear stealthy noises in the back-yard, pushed open the screen-door and pointed a rather etiolated beam of torchlight at Jim.

"W . . . who's there?" she demanded, with a queer, quavering truculence. Jim froze. Caught by surprise he could think of nothing more effective to do than to become a statue. A riot of vague pictures from his history lessons tumbled about in his mind—the Elgin marbles, the Laocoon, Hercules. . . . He stood stock still, bent forward, naked and precarious on top of the fence, goose-pimples of cold and terror popping out on his buttocks.

Mrs Hogan's yellow torch-beam fell short of him, but a diffused glow caught the fence and endowed Jim with a ghostly lack of substance—a kind of moonlit statuary in suburbia. Mrs Hogan suddenly spotted its vague whiteness and, with a sound that was both gurgle and gasp, retreated in terror. She stumbled to the phone and, after trying to dial with three fingers at once, finally got through to the police.

Meanwhile a scarred and panting Jim, having finished using the paling fence as a pedestal, hastily dragged the ladder into his yard and pushed it against the kitchen window. But when he climbed up to open it at last, the window wouldn't budge. Refusing to believe that it, too, had been locked by his all-suspecting mother, he rattled it furiously. But it held firm. He thumped again with his fists—and then realized with sudden fear that he was making more noise than Macduff knocking at the gates in Inverness. He shrank away from the window and crept down the ladder again. A spasm of shivering swept over him, and his teeth chattered.

Then he saw something. Standing upright in his father's backyard potato patch was a four-pronged garden fork—the perfect lever to wedge in under the stubborn window. He ran over, dragged it from the ground, and climbed back up the ladder. It was fairly easy to push the points of the prongs into the narrow slit between the frame and the window, but in his eagerness he didn't wedge them in far enough, so that when he bore down heavily on the handle, the tines suddenly splintered out of the wood and he all but dived headlong on to the gravel below. He saved himself by a frenzied and lucky clutch at the sill while the fork gonged like a bass tuning-fork against the concrete foundations beneath.

Jim hung there breathless for a second, but a spark of hope still glimmered with the moonshine on the tines. He descended, picked up the fork, and returned to the attack. This time he would make sure that he had the maximum possible purchase without the wood giving way. Twice he drove the tines in with what strength he could, but each time as he pressed down tentatively on the handle he felt them slipping out again. It would need a sudden vicious jab. He swung back and thrust the fork in sharply like a bayonet. But there were four points instead of one, and somehow the fork seemed to turn in his hand as he thrust. There was a grating crack, a clash of falling fragments as one of the tines struck glass instead of wood, and the window gaped emptily in front of him. Jim stared at it unbelievingly. Then he laughed—a sobbing laugh of incredulity and relief. For there was the opening! All he had to do was to crawl through it to safety and peace. In the morning he could get a pane of glass, fit it with tacks and putty, and there it was. Who would ever know?

A car raced up the street and stopped. Doors opened and footsteps hurried about the paths. Some went into Hogan's next door, and there was the sound of low and urgent consultation. Jim, still clutching the fork, crouched in the shadow on top of his ladder. The voices stopped and more footsteps crunched on the gravel. Some came over towards the fence and Jim froze against the wall in terror. Then, quite suddenly, a strong beam of light flashed on to him, and two policemen stood in the drive below.

"There he is!"

"Look out!"

"Move in slowly!"

"Watch that fork!"

Jim made a strangled sound as the policemen slowly moved in, never dousing the merciless glare of their torches for an instant. It didn't occur to him that a naked young man brandishing a digging fork on top of a ladder at midnight would scarcely look either modest or peace-loving. He felt ruthlessly exposed, a violent sense of intrusion, and tried unsuccessfully to hide behind the handle of the fork. At the same time he knew it was essential to say something reassuring, to explain the whole business simply and clearly. But the best he could manage was "I . . . I . . . " Two more policemen joined in the blockade and all four closed in steadily. They didn't say a word. Jim's mouth went on working until suddenly he surprised himself by announcing in a high squeak: "Look here, I'm Bear! Jim Bear!" The policemen either silently agreed or took it as a threat. For with a sudden rush they swept him from the ladder, flung off the fork, and bundled him unceremoniously on his back in the strawberry patch.

"Grab him!"

But at that moment Jim came violently to life. He leapt to his feet and sped round the house like a gazelle. The heavy sergeant pounded after him, and two of the younger policemen ran up the drive to try to head him off. But Jim had a clear lead. He shot across the lawn, took the front fence at a stride, and raced out on to the street almost under the wheels of a car. He and the car swerved simultaneously. There was a shriek of a woman and a screeching of tyres.

"It's *him*!" the woman screamed. "It's the peeping-tom!" There was a second of confusion as the police were cut off by the swerving driver. It was enough to give Jim the advantage. He swung back on to the footpath, hurdled Schuberts' fence next door, shot across their lawn, hurtled through two backyards, then doubled back and crouched behind the creeper that sprawled along his own back fence. Luckily at the same moment a dog barked further up the street. It unwittingly acted as a decoy, and the footsteps and voices of his pursuers faded away hurriedly towards it.

Jim stood up cautiously and listened. No sound. He peered over the fence into the backyard. No sign. The stepladder still stood by the gaping kitchen window, and the fork shone dimly in the garden strip below. Up to this point in his flight he had acted wholly by reflex and instinct; from the moment the policemen had appeared below him he hadn't planned so much as a gesture. But now his mind began working again, craftily. Doubling back on his tracks to outwit his pursuers, had been good strategy. He had often seen it done on TV, so why not in real life?

Stealthily he hauled himself over the back fence and dropped down into his own backyard. There he paused, breathing cautiously. No sound or movement. With sudden resolution he tip-toed across the back lawn, leapt the strawberry patch, ran lightly up the stepladder, and eased himself in through the broken window. The whole thing only took a couple of seconds. From the sill he lowered himself noiselessly inside, stepped gingerly for a yard or two, trying to avoid treading on broken glass, and then hurried down the darkness of the passage. His pyjamas were hanging on the bathroom rail. He put them on with a kind of breathless haste, the touch of clothing against his flesh suddenly filling him with a strange sense of security and gratitude. Then he padded quickly up to his room, got into bed, and pulled the bedclothes high up round his shoulders.

For a long time he lay there tingling and alert, his heart pounding and his breath panting heavily in spite of all his efforts to control it. He heard footsteps and voices returning. The heavy crunch of footfalls surrounded the house and congregated at the kitchen window. For a while a conference seemed to be going on there. Then they seemed to scatter over the neighbourhood again, all except one or two, who clumped up to the back door. A knock that frightened Jim to the marrow filled the dark house. He lay silently, holding his breath.

"Police here! Anybody home?" It was a big voice, as hard as authority, as stentorian as a trumpet. Jim felt that it was directed straight at him. The knock was repeated, terribly, shaking the door. "Police here! Anybody home?" Another interminable wait. Then at last the screen-door clumped shut and the footsteps faded towards the front gate.

Jim sat up in bed and listened at the window. "Nobody home," he heard the big voice say. "Either that, or they sleep like wet puddings." There was a lot of mumbling but although Jim strained his ears, he could only hear snatches of the conversation that made no sense to him. "Sex fiend," he heard several times, together with "breaking and entry," "nut" and "keep an eye on the place." He also heard the long trilling of a female voice—unmistakably Mrs Hogan's—telling the police how she was being terrorized by a lunatic, how Mr and Mrs Bear from next door had gone to Melbourne, and how their son Jim must be away for the week-end staying with his grandmother.

But at last the hubbub faded, doors slammed, and the police patrol cars cruised off slowly down the street. Jim lay back exhausted. It was after one o'clock in the morning; his flesh smarted from the raking scratches of the rose thorns, and his nerves ached from fear and tension. For a long time he couldn't sleep, and when he did doze off at last he fought his way panic-stricken through a series of nightmares in which he was playing a desperate game of football, naked, against a team of policemen armed with garden forks.

He woke with a start at half past seven, his mind a turmoil of fears and urgent thoughts . . . the window, the glass, the police, the football match. He dressed quickly, shuddering at the sight of himself in the mirror. He looked even worse than he had yesterday. Then he hurriedly swept up the broken glass in the kitchen. The stepladder was gone, so he supposed that either the police had shifted it, or Mr Hogan had come in to claim his property.

The thought of the police terrified him. They would be back shortly for certain, and he wanted to be off the place before they came. But first he had to mend the window. He measured the size of the frame, let himself out stealthily by the back door, and rode furiously down to Carter's Hardware Store. Old Mr Carter always opened at eight o'clock on Saturday mornings, and he kept a stock of glass in his store-room at the back of the shop. He was slow, but he was careful— and Jim was grateful for that, at least. Within half an hour he had returned, fitted the new pane into the frame, fastened it with brads, and sealed the edges with a bit of putty from his father's garage. He looked at the whole thing with pride; it was hard to tell that anything had ever happened to it.

He hurried inside, switched on the iron, and washed his hands. While he was snatching a bit of breakfast Ginger turned up, miaowing, at the back door.

"You blasted old mongrel," Jim growled as he let her in. "I ought to string you up after what you did to me last night." By the time he'd cut her meat the iron was sizzling with heat. He snatched up his football shorts, spread them hastily on the ironing board, and clumped the iron down square on the seat. To Jim it seemed that the iron barely touched the cloth before he lifted it again; and even allowing for the fact that he did glance round anxiously at Ginger who was beginning to hack and heave again, he could have sworn that the iron had not rested on his shorts for more than a second.

Yet when he lifted it away there was a brown scorch mark plumb across the seat of his pants. Against the white cloth it stood out like a huge autumn leaf. Horrified, Jim rushed to the sink, saturated the dish-cloth, and tried to sponge away the deep stain. But he had as much chance of washing it off as he had of rubbing the black smudges from his face.

"Holy cats!" he ejaculated. But there was nothing he could do about it. He switched off the iron, hastily smoothed out the worst of the wrinkles in his shorts, and tossed them into his kitbag with his boots and guernsey.

"Nice sort of galah a fellow'll look," he said testily to himself. "With a Hindu face and a pattern on his pants. At the big match and all."

He knew that at any minute the police might come back and the thought made him hurry. He put out the cat, grabbed his things, locked the door behind him, and rode quickly up the hill to the high school.

He didn't have as long to wait as he thought he would. Eddie Carter drifted into the dressing-shed before long, and so did Boomer and Harry Pearce. Boomer took a critical look at Jim. "Jees, you look a sight, Herc. Enough to frighten hell outa that East Adelaide mob before the match starts, even."

Jim had to steel himself. It was the kind of ridicule he'd have to learn to live with for weeks, perhaps months, until the silver nitrate stain slowly faded and disappeared. It was even worse when the teams took the field. The East Adelaide supporters naturally singled him out, and they didn't let up all day.

"Hey, Smallpox!" they shouted derisively. "You're

breaking out behind, too; did you know?" And they went off into shrieks of laughter. The constant barrage of heckling infuriated Jim, and he played like a demon. Fortunately the Hamilton supporters roared and cheered whatever he did—salve to his shame and anger.

It was a hard match, gladiatorial in fury; and at half time East Adelaide was a goal ahead.

"Come on, fellows! You can wrap them up with your hands behind your backs if you really try!" The coach was flailing about in the dressing-shed, shouting and exhorting. "Boomer, you take over full forward; Carter, go into ruck; and Bear, you switch to centre half forward." He checked the flow of his fiery oratory long enough to take a second look at Jim. "Hell, you look a sight, boy! But I doubt if it'll frighten the Bull, so watch him, boy; he's as heavy as a buffalo."

Despite the queer comparison, Jim knew what the coach meant. The Bull was the centre half back for East Adelaide, and he played like a tank. He had taken a particular dislike to Hamilton High, and especially to Jim, who was too fast for him.

"What's with this Smallpox?" he said to one of the local spectators. "He sick or somethin'?"

"Don't look too sick, the way he's playin'."

"I mean the face—all black and neurotic lookin'."

"Spilt stuff on it. Nitrate stuff."

"Yeah? Hot dog!"

"It'll wear off in time."

"Yeah? Then I better blacken it for 'im . . . real black."

The siren sounded, and the teams took the field for the last half. It was a torrid game. Goal for goal, point for point, they battled it out until only minutes remained. The time-keepers were crouched over their watches, the scorers checked their scores. Five points between the teams, East Adelaide in front. With two minutes left, the ball was see-sawing between the opposing back lines. A minute and a half, and it went into a scrimmage at centre. The umpire bounced, and the East Adelaide ruckman knocked prodigiously. One minute! The ball was swept towards the East Adelaide goal and the game seemed all over. But Ocky Olson took a desperate mark in defence and punted the ball back up the wing.

There it was carried forward in a flurry of play towards the centre again. Half a minute! Arms, hips, legs, boots, and bodies were milling about in a riot. Suddenly the ball shot out at an angle ahead of the crush, Ron Nelson aimed a kick at it from the ground, and it spun towards Eddie Carter. Fifteen seconds! Eddie swooped on it at centre half forward and passed towards Jim on the run. The ball went wide and bounced a yard in front of the Bull, but Jim chipped in like lightning ahead of him, swept up the ball with one hand, and straightened towards goal. Ten seconds! The Bull roared and flung out his huge arms, just missing Jim's waist with his tackle but crooking his fingers inside the top of his shorts. Jim's impetus carried him on, and the fabric, already weakened by washing and scorching, gave way with a terrifying rip. But Jim couldn't stop. The whole seat came away and the Bull was left holding it like a watch-dog with part of the postman in his teeth. A great roar went up as Jim hurtled on, the fluttering remnants of his pants somehow clinging miraculously to his waist. Five seconds! Jim bounced once, twice. He was clear of his opponents and almost within range. "Kick! Kick!" The ground echoed the roar, the stands rocked with it. The time-keepers reached for the switch. "Kick!"

Jim steadied for a second and let fly—a long, screwing punt that arched up in a high smooth trajectory and then curved downwards towards the goals. The siren sounded. It seemed to blare in a vacuum, hushed and unreal. There wasn't a human sound.

Then the ball gathered momentum in flight, curving in cleanly between the goal posts inches above the outstretched fingers of the defenders.

"A goal!"

The shout was stupendous, electrifying.

"A goal!"

"A goal!"

"We've won!"

Pandemonium! Chaos! Glory! Jubilation! Ecstasy! It was Hamilton High by a point, and Jim Bear was a hero above all heroes.

Even the headmaster overlooked his appearance, forgave him the silver-nitrate incident, and winked an eye at the immodest condition of his dress. Congratulations and celebrations bulged from the dressing-room. "By Jove, Jim," said the coach breathlessly. "You might have smallpox on your face and a flat iron on your bottom, boy, but you can kick goals when we need 'em. Well done, boy."

Jim was too gratified and exhausted to speak. The disasters and humiliations of Friday the Thirteenth were completely erased. He was invited home with Boomer to celebrate, and they spent the rest of the day recovering, and conducting post-mortems on the match. It was nearly five o'clock when Jim gathered up his things to go.

"Have to get tea for the cat and me," he said. "I'm baching!" Boomer was fascinated and envious. "No?"

"Yeah."

"Hot dog! How come?"

"Just happened."

"Don't happen to me."

Jim and Boomer suddenly thought of the same idea.

"Hey, come and stay with me."

"Both try bachin' together."

"Tonight."

Jim was delighted. It wouldn't be half so bad facing the empty house with Boomer. Company, security, friendship. It would be fun, really, even if the policemen called back.

Their houses were only three blocks apart. They walked the distance in a couple of minutes and then gorged a slap-up tea of canned beef stew and ice-cream.

"Nice cat," Boomer said politely, watching Ginger slurping her dish of milk.

"Stupid cat," Jim answered with sudden feeling.

"What's she done?" Boomer always came straight to the point.

"Ah-h, chuck it!" Jim said. "All cats are morons."

Boomer was nonplussed. "Yeah," he said noncommittally; "some people reckon they're sly too."

"Yuk!" It was Jim's sign for cutting off a conversation. "Better put her out now, Boomer. She'll be arching her back like the Sydney bridge in a minute, hackin' and heavin' all over the place."

"Yeah?"

"Yeah!"

Boomer put the cat out and shut the door.

They went down to the sitting room and watched football on television for a couple of hours, criticizing the form of the teams and debating the results of the finals. Then they listened to records, brewed hot chocolate, ate biscuits, watched a Western, and finally got ready for bed. Boomer held up his pyjamas. "Take a look at these, will you?"

Jim winced. "They a joke or something?"

"Some joke!"

"Did an old aunt give 'em to you for your birthday?"

"No aunt. Mum."

"She did?"

"Sure. Must hate me somethin' awful."

"Weird."

"Way out weird."

The pyjamas were a garish pattern of white and yellow stripes, a kind of ensign gone wild. When Boomer walked up the passage in them he looked like a sailor recently rescued from a wreck, wrapped in an unknown flag.

They climbed into bed at last, tired from talk and the excitement of the day. Within a couple of minutes Jim began to doze. He was in a cloudy presleep haze when he heard Boomer's voice, vague and querulous.

"What's that noise, Herc?"

"What noise?"

"Listen!"

Jim listened. Someone was tapping outside.

"Sounds like knocking," Boomer said.

Jim sat up suddenly. "Knocking?"

"Yeah."

Jim was out of bed in a second, fully awake. "Sounds like the window."

"Someone tryin' to break in, d'you reckon?"

"Holy cats!"

"Ring the cops."

"Cops?" The word stung Jim into new nervousness.

"No, wait." They both stood listening, straining to catch the sound.

"It's stopped."

"D'you reckon?"

"Can't hear anything."

"Might be finished."

"What d'you mean . . . finished?"

"Might've got the window open; might be inside already."

"Inside?"

"Listen! That's it."

Someone was tapping outside. Flap, flap, flap, it went, like a distressed fugitive slapping fast and hard at the window with the palm of his hand.

"Better see who it is," Jim said.

"Careful! Might be a . . . " Boomer trailed off indecisively.

"A what?" Jim stopped, hesitant. "A policeman?"

Boomer stared at him in disbelief. "A policeman? What the devil would a policeman be doing flapping around in the middle of the night?"

"Who, then?"

"Burglars, maybe. Mods, rockers, hoods. Might be the Bull."

"The Bull? What'd *he* want?"

"Do you over. Hates the sight of you after today's match; tear your insides out for gravy, he said he would."

Jim was aghast. "Listen! It's louder now."

"Better call the cops—quick, before they cut the wires."

"The teleph . . . They wouldn't do that."

"The Bull would!"

Boomer's fears and the threat of the severed wires

began to shake Jim. "Well . . . "

"Here, I will." Boomer padded up the darkened passage with a kind of elephantine stealth. "Dial OOO, isn't it? Emergency?" He dialled clumsily and waited, clutching the receiver. "Hullo? Quick, get me the police." He said it in the same urgent whisper he'd been using in the bedroom. Obviously the operator couldn't hear him. Jim heard Boomer gradually raising his voice: "Get me the police. . . . I said, get me the police. . . . I said, put me through to the police, please. . . . Police, please! Yes, police please." The operator at last got the message.

"Police?" Boomer said. "Listen, send a car to . . . what's your address, Herc?" in an urgent whisper . . . "to No. 6 Valencia Grove" (in a loud voice) . . . "and hurry. What for? Someone's breaking in. . . . Yes, breaking and entry. Yeah, that's it. Hurry."

He put down the receiver stealthily and dropped his voice back to a whisper. "Must be deaf in there! Be too bad if you were trying to warn 'em about a murderer in the house. Have to yell your head off to make 'em hear."

The word "murderer" raised the sense of uneasy tension again. They paused, listening.

"Any sound of him now?" Boomer asked.

"Seems further off."

"Round the side of the house. Listen!"

Jim's apprehension over the unknown intruder wasn't nearly as sharp now as his fear of the police—especially if they were the same squad who'd descended on the place the night before. He began trailing the sound by moving carefully from room to room. "It's outside the lounge room now," he whispered. "And it's low down against the wall." They listened. Flap,

flap, flap. The sound came through again, rather more softly and feebly.

"I think it's a thing, not a person."

Boomer was scarcely reassured. "A . . . a *thing*?"

"Yeah. Not human."

Boomer's nape tingled, and pictures of Dracula rose up out of the night. "*Not human!* Gor!"

But Jim was getting more matter-of-fact every minute. "I mean a creature. An animal or something."

Boomer's goose-flesh began to subside. "A . . . an animal? D'you reckon?"

"Listen!" The sound started again, gently, against the wall of the sitting room. Jim was suddenly very prosaic. "I'm going out to have a look."

"Careful, Herc."

Jim opened the front door slowly and stood listening. Complete silence. Boomer quaked and whispered very stealthily at his side: "They've heard us! Be ready in case they try to jump you."

An interminable wait. The wind stirred the shrubs gently. Jim stepped silently out on to the veranda and Boomer hesitated in the doorway behind him. "There it is!" They both whispered it together.

"That's not a person." Jim strode manfully to the corner of the veranda and peered quickly round it. There was a second's silence, then, "Oh no! Not you again!" The utter disgust and exasperation in his voice carried over to Boomer.

"W . . . what is it?"

"The blasted cat!"

"The cat?"

"With a bird."

"Well, damn me!"

"A starling or something. She's been playing tigers

with it, and the poor thing's been flopping and flapping against the wall with its wing. It's just about done for."

Jim aimed a barefooted kick at the cat. She leapt back and ran, bird in mouth, for the fence at the bottom of the garden. Boomer couldn't admit to himself that he'd been taken in. "The cat!" he kept saying. "The blasted cat!"

"At least she won't need any breakfast in the morning," Jim growled. "Not if she keeps mauling birds all night."

He turned back towards the corner of the house. The breeze stirred the hibiscus bush at the edge of the garden and momentarily flapped the bell-bottomed legs of Boomer's hysterical pyjamas. The front door creaked on its hinges for a second, then swung forward at gathering speed. Five yards away, Jim suddenly saw what was happening and leapt forward like a madman. "No! Oh no!" The door beat him by an instant. It slammed shut in his face with terrible finality, and the latch sprang in with a firm click.

"No! No!" He rushed at it, pushing and thudding with his knee. "My God!" he said. "It's done it again."

Boomer came up hastily, hopping grotesquely on one leg because his bare feet had unexpectedly encountered Mrs Bear's rose prunings. "What's up, Herc?"

Jim flung up his hands in agony. "Hellfire!"

"What?"

"We're locked out! That's what."

"Locked out? How?"

"By the door! By the blasted door!" Jim's anger flared up. But the seriousness of their plight slowly penetrated even Boomer's understanding. "Blow me," he said simply. "How do we get inside again?"

131

"You tell me," Jim said fiercely. He pushed futilely at the nearest window. "I don't know how Mum and Dad can manage to live in this place without getting themselves locked out every night. Darned if I do."

"Probably carry a key."

"In their pyjamas?"

"Maybe they don't go walking around much in their pyjamas." There was a simple logic about Boomer that Jim found intensely irritating. "Anyway, how do we get back in?"

"We can't," Jim said.

"What about the windows?"

"All locked."

"Mighty careful people, you Bears."

"You can say that again."

"Frightened of peeping-toms or something?"

"Mum is."

"S'pose we'll have to take a couple of tiles off, then."

"Tiles?"

"Yeah. From the roof."

"Can you take off tiles from the roof?"

"Sure. Dad's a tiler. I often help him—week-ends and holidays and that."

"Yeah, but what then?"

"Slip down through the manhole and open the door."

"No kidding?"

"Sure."

"Ever done it before?"

"Never had no need to."

Jim demurred. "How you going to get on the roof?"

"You got a ladder?"

"No, but Hogan . . ."

"Hogan what?"

Jim's voice seemed to grow very faint and small.

"The bloke next door's got one."

"Good, we'll borrow it."

Something inside Jim was trying to make a final desperate protest. "But the police . . . you rang them. . . ."

"They won't be here for a long time yet."

"But what if they . . . "

"We'll tell 'em the truth. No harm in that." Boomer, unaware of Jim's astounding escapade the night before, was supremely nonchalant, but to Jim it was all a fantastic nightmare. It seemed as if he was being carried along by events over which he no longer had any control.

At least there was no fence-climbing this time. Boomer merely led the way on tip-toe down Hogan's cement drive, manoeuvred the ladder stealthily out of the shed, and cajoled Jim into carrying it back between them.

"Where's the manhole, Herc, d'you know?"

"In the ceiling above the passage."

"Better get at it from the back, then."

Boomer propped the ladder against the guttering and climbed up gingerly in his bare feet. "Those rose cuttings of your mother's are a bit fierce, Herc. Beaks on 'em like fish-hooks."

But Jim was impatient of delays. "How many tiles d'you have to take off?"

"Half a dozen."

"What if it rains during the night?"

"Won't rain!"

"No? You spoke to old Hughie, I s'pose?"

"You holdin' that ladder?" Boomer looked back distrustfully.

"I got it."

133

"Sure?"

"Course I'm sure! Hurry up, will you! Nice couple of galahs we'd look if the police turned up now."

"Stop your whingein'. You got police on the brain, or somethin'?"

There was a faint wash of moonlight, and Jim had a view of Boomer silhouetted in strange perspective from the soles of his feet—the tall, striped tubes of his pyjama trousers stretching up and away towards the roof. He was so concerned with looking upwards and trying to hear what was happening to his father's tiles that he had no thought for anything else.

Boomer struggled and grunted for a while, then looked back down the ladder. "Pass me up a bar or something, will you, Herc. I've got to lever the first one up a bit."

"What sort of bar?"

"Anything. That fork'll do."

"Just a second."

Jim bent down, picked up the fork, and held it high above his head so that Boomer could bend down and reach it.

"*There he is!*"

A torch snapped on like an arc-light, and Jim was caught suddenly in a kind of photographic pose, like a javelin thrower in the arena.

"It's the same one!" The voice was hard, accusing.

"Careful, he's dangerous!"

"Mind that fork!"

"Mental case!"

"Close in slowly."

Jim was caught off guard for only a second. Then he leapt away like a springbok. "Run for your life!" he yelled. The ladder slipped back off the guttering and Boomer began a downward swoop from the upper rungs like a dogman riding a falling girder to earth. His legs were already running when they were still three feet from the ground. He didn't question why he and Jim were fleeing, or from what. Jim's wild yell, and the sight of the encircling policemen, were enough. It was just an overpowering urge, a sense of mortal danger behind them and fierce flight in front.

The falling ladder checked the police momentarily, and enabled Jim and Boomer to elude their lunge. Then the two pyjama-clad figures were away. They vaulted the back fence like acrobats, flashed across two back-yards, crossed the first street, plunged over a vegetable garden, and raced through a row of carports and open verandas.

"Quick, this way. Head for home." Boomer seemed to take the right route by instinct. They avoided the open streets and hurtled across lawns and backyards. Behind them the hue and cry of pursuit rose and spread.

"Pol . . . police was it, Herc?" Boomer panted in a whisper.

"Yeah, police."

"Go . . . gonna arrest us . . . it looked like . . . Herc."

"Arrest us for sure."

"Better shoot home to bed . . . never find us there. Next block up, our house."

Mrs Prudence Ey, of 17 Winchester Street, was just going to bed when she remembered that she'd left the bucket of oranges from her father's orchard standing at the back door. It had to be brought inside. She padded out through the lean-to veranda in her night-gown, switched on the backyard light, and stepped out into the immodest night air. As she did so, two figures in pyjamas rushed across the lawn beside her, almost knocking the bucket from her hand, leapt the side fence at a stride, and disappeared across O'Shaughnessy's yard next door.

Mrs Ey screamed very shrilly. "It's him! It's him!" Her husband leapt down the passage to save her.

"It's him! The tom! The peeping-tom!"

"Where? Where?"

"Two of them! Two toms! In pyjamas."

"Where?"

"In the backyard! Ring the police, Mervin! Ring the police! Quick!" They both rushed inside, Mrs Ey trembling like a junket.

"I seen 'em both, plain as daylight! A half-caste, one of 'em was, spotty and 'orrible, with a escaped convict beside 'im, runnin' like mad."

Her husband dialled the police, all fingers at once.

Meanwhile the half-caste and the convict had raced across all the backyards in the block, their figures gradually diminishing in the thin moonlight, vaulting the fences like distant fleas, fading and merging into the hazy gloom. Behind them the noise of pursuit died away, and Adelaide's vast suburban sea sighed itself slowly back to sleep.

At No. 6 Valencia Grove the policemen took a long time to disperse. But they drove away at last, and the house settled back into silence like its neighbours. From the shelter of the hibiscus bush by the corner of the garden Ginger, the big tortoiseshell cat, emerged slowly and stalked up on to the veranda. She arched momentarily against the wrought iron legs of the garden seat there, yawned hugely, and gazed out with disdain at the dullness of the world around her. Then she curled up on the mat at the back door and went to sleep.

Dad Ran A Fowl Run

DAD kept fowls once and I'll never forget it. Dad won't forget it either, though in his more expansive moments afterwards he always claimed that Mum had egged him on—and then pointed the pun with one of those incomparable winks of his that had the subtlety of a badly operated tip-truck.

Yet perhaps Mum really was to blame, for it all started from a remark of hers one August morning when we were half-way through breakfast. Dad's eyes were peering pugilistically from under their eyebrow verandas at the dismal scene outside. A drab sky was sagging down on an even drabber sea of grey mallee that flowed on drearily to the horizon; and nearer at hand the frowzy straw roofs and unmortared lime-stone sides of the sheds and stables peeped and pried and struck attitudes among the trees in the yard. Cow-shed, pig-sty, hay-stack, bull-shed, straw-stack, horse-stable, seed-barn . . . these, and their haphazard screen of knuckle-rooted mallees looked, both in situation and condition, as if they'd been dropped at random from a low-flying aeroplane.

A dry, probing easterly was stirring the drift-sand and ruffling the feathers of the fowls in the fowl-proof garden. I had often looked down on it all from the windmill tower on mornings like this. With the smoke streaming from our thrust-forward kitchen, the house looked like an overworked paddle steamer trying to tow a clutch of unruly and half-submerged barges through the mallee sea. Perhaps it was the sight of these; perhaps it was the winter drought and the prospect of an even bigger overdraft. Anyway, Dad was in one of those difficult moods that kept Mum hopping and twittering between breadboard and teapot. He had just finished devouring six eggs and was wiping his plate aggressively with a chunk of naked bread.

"Any more eggs?" he demanded.

"No!" Mum said apologetically. "You never have more than six."

"Wouldn't hurt to have a few spares," Dad told her. "Keep them round the place for cold mornings like this."

Mum promised to create such a reserve in the kitchen in future, instead of keeping her whole egg reservoir down in the cellar as she did now. Then, as if suddenly emboldened by the threat of drought and debt, she blurted out, "Six ought to do you, all the same, Alfred. That would cost you four shillings if you lived in Adelaide."

"I don't live in Adelaide," Dad said uncompromisingly. "And I'm not likely to. I've got more sense."

Mum stuck to her guns. "All the same, people in Adelaide have to buy them at that price. And if we didn't eat so many, they could buy *ours*."

Dad was getting impatient, the more so because Mum's argument so far was undeniable. But when Mum was on a scent she stuck to it. "If we all had six eggs each," she said, looking round at the seven of us—five boys and Louisa and Betty, "it would be over four dozen every morning. And that would cost us ten pounds a week."

Perhaps it was the way Mum spoke, or just the sheer enormity of the figures, even allowing for her arithmetic, that suddenly shocked Dad into silence. He pushed back his chair and strode down to the blacksmith's bellows under a big rooty mallee. There he worked several sums in the drift-sand with a long thin stick and looked contemplatively at a rusty cultivator that was leaning on its side by the old fowl-house and thrusting up one of its levers like a prophetic finger at a fowl perched in the tree above. It was obvious that Dad was conceiving an Idea, but we all knew better than to disturb him during the period of gestation. Only Bruno, the eldest of us and something of a rebel, dared voice the general uneasiness. "He's got something on his mind," he said to Herb and me after lunch. "So you'd better be careful. It'll fall heavy."

It fell at tea-time.

"I've been thinking," Dad said, and there was a deep silence into which the announcement set and mortared itself like a foundation for the things to come. "We ought to keep more fowls."

"Oh, Alfred!" Mum spoke with the spontaneity and genuine pleasure of one who sees the exaltation of the meek and humble. "That'll be wonderful. We'll be able to sell the eggs before they're eaten."

We all saw Mum's point, but kept our eyes on Dad, because in our house all things, both good and bad, came from him.

"Yes, I've worked it out. We could keep five hundred fowls with no trouble at all. They'd just run around the place and fossick like the ones we've got now. No expense, no machinery, no wages. . . ."

Bruno opened his mouth but closed it again without speaking.

"Each one ought to lay an egg a day," Dad went on statistically. "So with five hundred fowls that would be three and a half thousand eggs a week. That's nearly three hundred dozen," he added illuminatingly, "and they'd be worth a hundred pounds."

A hundred pounds a week! And for nothing. The thought staggered Mum and Bruno and Louisa and the rest of us who already knew what money—or the lack of it—meant. I'm not sure that it didn't stagger Dad too. Certainly he began to eye all the stray fowls about the place with a look of mingled wonderment, respect, and avarice; and at breakfast his assault on his six eggs was not nearly so hearty as it had been before.

Bruno, of course, was suspicious. "S'pose they *don't* lay an egg a day," he said. "What then?"

"I've thought of that," said Dad. "Even six a week would do—just half a dozen. That way we'd get 250 dozen a week."

Mum murmured her earnest approval of such a concession, and Dad warmed to her magnanimously. "After all," he said, "why shouldn't a fowl have a day off like the rest of us? We have Sundays. We wouldn't like to be laying an egg every day all the year round, I'll bet."

A faint smirk round the corner of Louisa's mouth showed that she couldn't imagine Dad laying an egg on *any* day of the week; he was altogether too big, cumbersome, and featherless for such an essentially feminine act. But she, too, knew better than to interrupt Dad in the middle of a new idea, and so we all conceded Sunday as a holiday for hens, and heard him out while he flooded our minds with fowls, feathers, and pound notes.

The first practical step in the campaign was taken the next morning. Dad mustered all of us in an imposing line and led us down among the mallee trees in the yard, where he began pacing distances with the long measured stride of a deliberating philosopher.

"We'll put up the shed here," he said. "And the sooner the quicker."

"I thought you said the new fowls could just run around the place anywhere, like the old ones," said Bruno truculently; "so what do you want to build a shed for?"

"Use your head, boy!" Dad showed the impatience that is the privilege of superiority. "We mightn't need a shed for them to *sleep* in, but we'll need one for them to *lay* in, or there'll be eggs lying about everywhere for the hawks and dogs to eat, and damn fool visitors to step on."

Bruno was unperturbed. "Then you'll have to make nests . . . for the fowls to lay in."

Dad looked up sharply at the mocking blend of derision and laughter in Bruno's voice, but as there was no hint of disrespect in his face he let it pass. "Of course we'll make nests. That's what the shed's for. We'll use old boxes and things."

"Lots of nests," said Bruno. "Dozens of nests."

"A dozen'll do."

"At least fifty."

"To hell with it," cried Dad. "Who's building this shed?"

Herb and I started to edge out of the buffer zone between Dad and Bruno as soon as we saw the likelihood of hostilities.

"You'll still need fifty nests," said Bruno doggedly.

"What about building a separate shed for each hen?" Dad said, his passion rising to sarcasm; "with a sleep-out for the rooster."

"Fifty nests," intoned Bruno, "for five hundred fowls . . . ten fowls to a nest. . . ."

Dad wavered as if a hand had suddenly brushed

before his eyes, and Bruno took advantage of it.

"Ten fowls to a nest. If you have more they'd never fit. As it is, ten's too many if they all want to lay at the same time."

"Then some of them can bloody well wait!" Dad was in no mood for compromise.

"Form a queue, like!" Bruno always played Dad mood for mood.

"Don't talk stupid! Ten fowls won't all be wanting to use the same nest at the same time."

"If they want to lay an egg they will. They can't be waiting around outside crossing their legs and clicking their toes while some other hen finishes. When you're laying an egg you can't wait." The veins on the side of Dad's nose were starting to bulge, but he restrained himself by letting his anger leak into sarcasm again.

"And when was the last time you laid one? That old soft-shell Herb wouldn't eat for breakfast?"

In the end they compromised at twenty boxes, and Bruno accepted the inevitability of fowl queues and random nests in the scrub.

And so we went to work. Mallee uprights and crossbeams, thatched walls of mallee branches, straw roof; out of the bare ground rose our fowl coop, with tier on tier of crooked sticks and wire for roosts, until the whole thing looked like a wartime beach trap or badly constructed wire entanglement.

"Ah," said Dad with satisfaction, "they'll like that! You wait." But Bruno was still disgruntled. "All we need now," he said, "is some fowls to put in it."

"We'll have fowls!" Dad waved his hand airily as if about to conjure them down in flocks from the branches of the encircling scrub. "And ducks," he added triumphantly; "we'll have ducks too."

Bruno rested on his crowbar, pushed back his hat, and gave Dad a look of such utter incredulity that Herb half burst into a riotous whoop, checked himself under the fury of Dad's eye, and turned away with his mouth still twisted in its guffaw like a frozen flounder's.

"Ducks?" Bruno said unbelievingly. "Ducks?"

And indeed, of all the monstrous notions ever suggested by Dad, this seemed the most completely lunatic. Ducks in this Gomorrah of drift, flies, and sand-blast! Or was Dad, like some ancient, shaggy Elijah, going to lure them down out of the sky—the wild fowl of the air? The disbelief on our faces must have been comic, because even Dad unbent suddenly, chuckled knowingly, and marched off ahead of us.

"Bring the shovels and the wheelbarrow," he said over his shoulder, "and I'll show you."

Our faces fell, and Bruno drove the crowbar down on a piece of limestone with a curse.

"Crazy nonsense and be damned to it," he said, out of Dad's earshot. "If it's a duckpond he wants, he can dig it himself."

For a few minutes we shared Bruno's dreadful suspicion, but as Dad led us down past the house towards the road we suddenly came upon the truth. It was the Government Tank—an old underground reservoir vital in the summers of a generation ago, but since made obsolete by the great mains from down south and now quite derelict and neglected. Its low masonry walls rose up from below and sat squat on the earth like an abandoned pillbox, and its intake vent gaped and mouthed at the overgrown drain that was meant to fill it. The run-off from the road in our rare times

143

of rain had proved that it was a mud trap of an advanced design . . . as well, of course, as a potential duckpond for Dad.

"Dump a bit of stuff this end," he said, standing like Napoleon on the crumbling ramparts, "and you can make a ramp to wheel the rest of the muck out."

"Ducks *like* mud," Bruno said.

"Yes, but they like water better; they can swim in that."

"Where are you going to get the water from, I'd like to know."

"Don't talk stupid! The winter rains will fill it in a day once we've cleaned out the drain."

"The winter's over and there hasn't been any rain yet."

"Get the barrow!" Dad hated heresy. "You're as bad as Oscar Aveling . . . do nothing but talk."

Bruno sullenly joined the rest of us and we started the job of shifting enough mud to make room for an equivalent volume of ducks.

"Damn stupid," Bruno muttered. "Where is he going to put the things until it rains? In the bath-tub?"

"You can go and finish it tomorrow," Dad said patriarchally; "and the drain too, if you get time. I'm going in to Gonunda in the morning to see what the market is like."

"It'll take a month," said Bruno. "Better get a bull-dozer while you're there."

We were all waiting round the tea-table the next night when Dad arrived back. Even before he flung open the door we knew from the crashing of gates and wash-basins that the Stasinowskis had fallen upon evil times. Mum blanched and cut so furiously and blindly at the bread that the pile of slices was six inches high before Dad burst in, strode to his place, and sat down breathing hairily through his nostrils. There was an awesome silence.

"Alfred, did . . . did you get the fowls?" Mum ventured meekly at last. Dad glowered out from underneath his beetling brows and swept us with a glare like a blowlamp.

"Rogues," he said succinctly. "Lowdown, thieving rogues."

"W-what did they do, Alfred?"

"They sold fowls, that's what they did." He gave one of his dreadful ironical laughs. "But not to me. I'd see them roasted first—fowls and all."

"W-what did they say to you?"

"What did *I* say to *them*," Dad began, but our leaping imaginations did the rest. He paused and took a fierce gulp of boiling tea.

"Do you know what they wanted for their fowls—scrawny fox-fodder that they were?"

We hung on his words, breathless.

"Ten shillings each!" Dad gazed at us, incensed, outraged, scandalized. "Ten shillings each!" He took another gulp of tea. "And d'you know what that would add up to for our five hundred?" He paused to allow our arithmetic time to catch up. "Two hundred and fifty pounds." Aghast, he looked from one of us to the other. "Two hundred and fifty pounds! For a few hens." He was beyond words and gave expression to the rest of his feelings by a terrible and sustained attack on the cold meat and potatoes on his plate.

Perhaps if he had left it at that all might still have been well. But his pride was stung and the drought worsened; and, worst of all, old Oscar Aveling came riding down the road a few days later and saw us still cleaning out the tank. He came over, gazed about searchingly for a long moment, and spat reflectively and unerringly down on Herb's shovel.

"Heard you was after some fowls, Stas," he said. "What sort did you want?"

"At that price," Dad said, rumbling, "I don't want any."

"Don't blame you," said old Oscar sympathetically. "Only a madman or a millionaire buys things when he don't have to." Dad looked up sharply. "What d'you mean?"

"I mean you needn't buy fowls at all."

"Well?"

"You can *breed* 'em."

"How?"

"Out of eggs . . . how else?"

The suspicious gloom rose slowly from Dad's face like the shadow of a cloud passing up a ridge. It was the nearest I'd ever seen him come to gratitude, at least where old Oscar was concerned.

"Breed 'em! Blow me, I'd never thought of that."

"Easy. Done it meself, often."

"You have? With clucks?"

"Nah!" Oscar gobbed at a stone in disgust. "Clucks ain't reliable. Comes a bit of rain or a new rooster or a change in the weather and they'll uncluck again as quick as you like. Then what can you do—sit on the eggs yourself? And they're so clumsy with it— roll 'em out, scratch, fight, and then leave 'em altogether a day before they're due. . . . Nah, clucky hens is worse than clucky women."

"Well, what then? How can you breed?"

"Incubator."

"Incubator?"

"Nothing simpler."

"Damn me!"

"Never misses."

"You got one, Oscar?"

"Sure thing. Beauty. Holds ten dozen. Four batches, and you'd have your five hundred."

"Would you be willing to . . ."

"Yeah, I'll hire it to you, Stas. Pound a month."

"Pound a month?"

"Fair enough, ain't it? You get a hundred hens for the price of two . . . add a bit of kerosene to keep things going."

"Thanks," said Dad. "Fair enough."

"And I'll let you have the eggs if you like. At market price. It's a good breed I've got, too."

Two days later Dad started incubating. Fortunately old Oscar came over to supervise the installation and initial lighting up, so there was no serious hitch in the opening ceremony. Dad at first was all for having the incubator in the dining room where, he said, he could keep an eye on it through the night, but Mum and Louisa wouldn't hear of it. So in the end he had to barricade part of the back veranda and set up his hatchery there. For the first few days it was such a fascinating sport that we kept lining up for the privilege of gazing through the glass peephole at the rows of white silent eggs balancing there on end like a Swan Lake chorus, and we argued about the thermometer reading fiercely down to the nth degree. Dad tolerated this at first much as a reclining tiger tolerates the climbing and tumbling of his own cubs. There was something theatrical about the way he turned the eggs, trimmed the wick, and checked the kerosene supply. In his way Dad was no mean showman: his adjusting of the temperature smacked of the conjurer or magician, and we watched engrossed as the distant flame rose like a cobra or sank silently to his will.

But time dragged after a while, even for Dad, and he mumbled and mouthed over his calendar with growing impatience.

"Don't know how a hen can put up with it," he blurted out one morning. "Damned if I do."

Mum was mildly shocked. "Oh, Alfred, don't talk nonsense. It is only three weeks, the whole thing."

"Who'd like to sit down on his behind for three weeks though, on a nest full of eggs."

"The hens don't notice that," Mum said, almost blushing at the thought. "It's just nature. Some things take a lot longer than three weeks."

"Well," Dad said with a look of sublime resignation, "all I can say is that it's a good thing elephants don't lay eggs." Mum didn't follow.

"If they did," Dad said, elucidating, "some fool idiot like me would try to hatch 'em . . . and then I'd be peepholing for years."

But at last the collective birthday arrived. Dad was beside himself as the first chick finally broke free after a convulsive struggle and lay there on its side looking like a wet, much-licked piece of cat's fur. I'm sure that we, his human offspring, born as we were to midwives and nursing homes, never held our father's rapt attention as that chicken did. There had been no glass partition for us as there was for it, and no Dad like this—bent double and creaking at the joints, thrusting his eyes along the glass like a pup peering through the slot of a letter-box.

An hour or two later he came triumphantly into

the kitchen carrying the chicken like a puff of yellow wattle in the great calloused cup of his hands. He walked mincingly, with his shoulders thrust forward as if the chicken he carried was in as much danger of being trodden underfoot as it was of being crushed to death in his hands.

"Look at that," he said. "It's alive! The first one."

"Oh, Alfred," Mum cried, beaming. "And without a cluck, too."

"Except Dad," said Bruno. "For ten dozen eggs you have to have a very big cluck."

Dad wheeled on him heavily, but Bruno knew when he'd gone too far, and the door closed on him almost before the words were out.

For two halcyon days the miracle of bird-birth was all around us, and Dad's heart was as full as his hands. The incubator jostled with yellow chickens—fifty or more in a milling mass, rocking unstably from beak to tail, stumbling and cheeping, propped sideways on their flipper-wings like little outriggers. But unhappily Dad's joy was short lived. On the third day the total rose by only two, and on the fourth, several having died overnight, it actually decreased. Anna, only just eight and the youngest of us, was distressed.

"When are the rest of the eggs going to hatch out, Dad?" she asked.

Dad rumbled in his boots. "I wish I knew."

"Why do some hatch quicker than others?"

"The shells must be harder."

"So it's harder for the poor chick to get out?"

"Yes. Now run away, Anna."

"How does the chick get inside the egg, Dad?"

"Never mind! Run away and don't worry me."

"Why do the chicks hatch out in the ink-you-baker but not in the cellar or the dairy?"

"Run away and play, I said."

"Which ones are boy chicks and which ones are girls?"

"Get the hell out of here. . . ."

But Anna had gone. Like Bruno she, too, could judge Dad to a nicety. Perhaps she picked up some of the rudiments of life that night when Dad dragged the incubator into the kitchen and made his final check of the unhatched eggs. He took each one in turn, examined it minutely for cracks—probably less as a guide to imminent birth than as a precaution against the treatment he was about to give it—and then shook it with incredible speed and ferocity, very much as he shook the salt cellar when he wanted to warn Mum that it was empty or clogged up.

"Rotten!" he would say with terrible finality, and Mum, hearing the gurgling fluid rush and flop from end to end, blanched before his smouldering fury and the hideous possibility that at any minute one of the eggs might slip from his fingers. But the pile grew speedily without mishap to the last shaking and the last rejection.

"Fifty-six," Dad said with a slow deliberation that was always ominous. "Nearly as many rotten eggs as chickens."

"Whatever could have been the matter," Mum said, pained. "They were all good eggs . . . all from Oscar Aveling."

"Good eggs my eye! That's the last time that swindler sells me anything. I've got half a mind to walk over and let him have these back—straight through the front door."

"But why should so *many* be bad . . . nearly half of them?"

"Because," Dad snorted, "his roosters are about as useful as old Oscar is himself. Anyone can see that."

"But he had a rooster specially sent up from Adelaide; a real fine bird; a pedigreed bird."

"Huh! City stuff! You can never rely on city stuff. You judge by results."

"Yes, Alfred," Mum said, blushing at the trend of Dad's talk.

"In future we use our own eggs," Dad said, "and Oscar Aveling can stick his up his jumper."

"Yes, Alfred," said Mum. "I'll get a batch ready tomorrow."

Despite the creeping fire of Dad's anger we were secretly delighted at the outcome of the first brood. There had been enough chickens to interest and entertain us all, and now we had over four dozen rotten eggs to dispose of. Bruno, Herb, and I—being boys and old enough to assume such responsibility—were officially charged by Mum with their destruction, after having been briefed like a bomb-disposal squad about the dangers involved, and the need for extreme care. Bruno was all for storing a dozen or two in the implement shed until the next election or until some spruiker from a travelling circus came up to Gonunda.

"We could even keep a few in reserve until the next agent comes round pestering us again," he said, "and as soon as Dad boiled over we could let fly."

But Herb and I were too impatient for such strategy and, having once felt the exultation of grenade-throwing with rotten eggs, we soon thirsted for more ammunition. It was all that Bruno could do to dissuade us from using fresh eggs when the supply from Mum had run out.

During the next three weeks we waited impatiently for Dad's second incubation, hoping that the percentage of chickens hatched would not rise too sharply. In actual fact he brought out eighty, but cats, hawks, falling weights, doors, gates, and sharp October frosts killed three dozen of them during the first six weeks, so that the two hatchings together netted no more than a hundred scrawny, gangling young birds by the time Christmas came round. But in spite of all this Dad was not dispirited. Within twelve months, he calculated, at this rate he would have his five hundred fowls and his hundred pounds a week. And up to date the grand enterprise had cost him comparatively little because now Mum supplied the eggs from her own fowls, and the kerosene came from her lamp drum. So it was March or April before the first real miscalculation in Dad's scheme became clear. For of the hundred young birds scratching about near the hen house, at least half soon showed that they would never lay an egg in a year, let alone six a week. They were cockerels.

"Roosters!" Dad said in disgust. "Blasted roosters! Combs on them like false teeth."

Mum tried in vain to pacify him. "You must have some of each, Alfred."

"I want eggs! And roosters don't lay eggs."

"You can sell them, or use them for soup."

Dad wasn't interested. "Isn't there any way of telling before the eggs go into the incubator?"

"They say if you dangle a needle over each one you can tell by the way the needle swings. Martha Kumiss says she can do it for animals and people."

"That's a lot of bunkum!"

"We could try it with Blossom; she calves next week."

"How the devil are you going to get her to lie down in the bail while you dangle a needle over her belly? Talk sense, woman." Mum's suggestion having been dealt with, the matter of predetermining a chicken's sex was dropped.

Dad's second problem came when the pullets at last began to lay. Old Harry Mader, the grocer in Gonunda, shook his head wisely at Dad.

"Too small, Stas; too small altogether. I couldn't hardly let them go through with the ungraded."

"Well, dammit, they'll get bigger."

"Ah, but *when*, Stas? You should think of that before you start breeding. Breed a big strain; get a good big rooster or two, and some fine breeding hens, and you'll have two-ounce eggs right from the start. Pay for the extra expense in a week."

"Perhaps you're right," said Dad.

"Of course I am right," Harry said, warming to himself. "Look at the low price you're going to be getting for these pigeons' eggs of yours . . . if you can get rid of them at all."

"But where can I get a good rooster like that?"

"Well, now," said Harry, "it's just a stroke of luck. My brother is sending up some next week, and I'll get him to put in two extra for you. Giants of birds; you can't hardly lift 'em."

"How much?" asked Dad.

"Three guineas each."

"Three guineas! Hell, I'd want an emu for that price."

Old Harry spread out his arms and shrugged his

shoulders so hard that his head disappeared into his coat, like a turtle's.

"There it is, Stas. Take it or leave it."

Dad took it. The two roosters came up to Gonunda by train the following week. Old Harry was on the station to introduce them when we arrived. "Feel the weight," he said, sagging under a massive crate. "It's enormous."

The two birds blinked their shutters with unbelievable speed, and croaked alarmingly deep down in their throats.

"They'd better be good," Dad said, shouldering the box. "I want eggs like footballs after this."

There followed a quiescent period until the spring, and then there came the inevitable quickening and burgeoning. The underground tank, filled at last by stormwater from the road, stank abominably of ducks; the two imported roosters stamped their likenesses vigorously on eight dozen sturdy new chicks—the most successful brood in all Dad's endeavours; and exactly a year after the beginning of his grand idea Dad, though still a little short of his hundred pounds a week, was at least making ten.

And then, out of imminent success, came disaster. We first sensed the evil by overhearing Harry Mader in his grocery shop, though it came merely as the confirmation of a month's uneasy suspicion that something was wrong.

"Old Stas's got it now," Harry said to Carl Kumiss; "have you heard?"

"Got what?"

"Stickfast and the tick, both."

"Both?"

"Poor devil! He didn't even know till yesterday."

"He didn't?"

"Not till yesterday. But it's been going on for months. I showed him; just happened to be out there delivering sheep-dip."

"You sure it's the tick?"

"Course. Real bad. Them two prize roosters I got for him—combs are whiter than my night-shirt; not enough strength to jump over a grain of wheat, hardly."

We hastened to tell Dad, but of course he already knew and silenced us brusquely. "Pests and diseases," he said bitterly; "enough to send a man off his head."

We weren't sure whether we ourselves had been included in a sort of blanket definition that covered all evils indiscriminately.

"Always something wrong, always something to drench or dip or spray or pickle. Smut, rust, black spot, toxaemia, codlin moth, mildew, milk-fever, maggots. . . . It's a wonder that a man can live, that he hasn't got borers drilling into his insides and insects gnawing at his back."

"He can if he wants to," Bruno said. "Flies and fleas and lice, and when he's dead, worms. . . ."

"Don't talk stupid!" Dad was in a dangerous mood, the more so because for once he was nonplussed. "How do you get rid of these ticks?" he asked desperately. "You can dip the fowls, I s'pose, but you can't dip the shed. And that'll be swarming with the blood-sucking vampires."

"Burn it down," Bruno said, "and build a new one."

"Talk sense or don't talk at all." Dad was edgier than he'd been for weeks.

Luckily for us old Oscar Aveling came ambling down the track that evening as he always did whenever we had fallen on evil times.

"Hear you got the tick, Stas," he said, taking aim at the bottom hinge of the gate and spitting with his usual accuracy.

"Yes," Dad said.

"They'll kill your fowls; least, they'll stop 'em laying, so you won't get any eggs either way."

"What I want to know is how to kill *them*."

"The ticks?"

"Yes."

"Easy. Had 'em myself three times."

"You did?"

"Course. My fowls, not me."

"Did you get rid of 'em?"

"Easy."

"How?"

"Cyanide."

"Cyanide! Hell, that's a bit strong, ain't it?"

Old Oscar thrust one hand into his breast and assumed a superior attitude. "Cyanide is the only thing."

"How do you get it?"

"Go and see Bert Thompson; he'll give you a bag full. And if he won't, I've still got plenty you can have."

"What do you do with it when you've got it?"

"Just sprinkle it all over the ground where they roost, and rake it in a bit."

"That all? Sounds easy."

"'Tis easy." Oscar adjusted his legs. "Course you have to be a bit careful."

The following afternoon Dad began what Herb called Operation Tick. Equipped with rakes, shovels, dusting dippers, and a big tin of cyanide powder, he clumped down to the fowl-house. The two roosters and twenty or more hens sat moodily on the roosts or jostled weakly in the corner. Dad shut the door and arranged his apparatus.

"Never mind, you stupid henheads," he muttered. "We'll soon fix these blood-suckers!" And with a vigorous swishing of the body he scattered the powder and began raking powerfully.

It was some moments before Herb and I, watching through the wire netting, guessed that something unscheduled was afoot. The bigger of the two roosters suddenly swayed sickeningly on his perch, opened his beak imploringly for an instant, and then fell with a meaty thud and lay there gasping. A moment later his companion's head lolled over like a wilting stem and, with a guttural *garkhh*, he thudded down at Dad's feet too, with the dirty parchment-like shutter of his eye slowly sliding down. Then, in quick succession, singly and in twos and threes, most of the fowls flopped over and did the same.

Dad straightened up, entangling himself violently in the fowl-roosts as he did so, but he fought free, flung down the rake, and reeled unsteadily to the door. Herb and I ran to him and dragged him, lurching and sagging, towards the house. Mum screamed and bore down on us hysterically, snatching and gesticulating, but the moment we surrendered Dad to her she dropped him all over the veranda and we had to prop him up against the wall by the kitchen door. It was the first time I had ever seen Dad as anything other than a kind of Hercules, and his sudden weakness terrified me.

"My head," he said vaguely, holding it tightly in both hands. "It's split right down the middle like a watermelon."

Mum gave another fluttering shriek and all but

collapsed beside him. The picture of any head split symmetrically was too much for her—that, and the suggestion of soft red flesh given out by the thought of the watermelon.

"It's split clean in two," murmured Dad. "And now someone's banging the two pieces together. Ohhhh!"

We all shuddered horribly, but Louisa, the most practical of all in an emergency, came running out with a cold wet towel, wiped his face with it, and wrapped it round his head. Slowly the clashing of the two halves changed to a sledgehammer striking from above, so Dad told us, which gave place in turn to a mallet, and finally a mere tack hammer. But it was two days before the ache left him and he felt fit to live again. And then, naturally, his first target was old Oscar. It was already late afternoon but that didn't stop Dad.

"Quick," Mum cried out to Bruno, Herb, and me. "Run after him; he'll kill poor Mr Aveling, he'll kill him."

Old Oscar met us amiably at his front gate and was completely taken aback by Dad's opening onslaught. "A man ought to sue you."

"What?"

"Or maybe make a nose-bag for you, you blasted old crow."

"What are you talking about, Stas?"

"Fill it with cyanide and push your head in it."

"Hey, what's up?"

"Cyanide!" Dad rose to sarcasm. "Kills tick, don't it?"

"Course it kills tick."

Dad suddenly thrust his face forward so far that old Oscar had to back away to get it into proper perspective again.

"Course it kills tick," Dad echoed with terrible derision. "And I'll tell you damn well how, you old mongrel."

"Here, Stas, stop that! I'll take the horsewhip to you."

"By killing the poor bloody chooks they're feeding on, that's how."

"The stock whip, that's what I'll take. . . . *What*?"

"What I said."

"You killed the chooks?"

"You heard! Touch and go killed myself too. Manslaughter it would have been; a fellow ought to run you in . . . you're not safe to be loose."

"I said to be careful."

"I *was* careful, damn you! You ought to be put away."

"I s'pose you swallowed the stuff."

"I did what you said."

"What did I say?"

"Sprinkle it where they roost and rake it in."

"That's what I do, exactly."

"Then how is it my fowls all fall down dead, and yours don't?"

"Because they're weaklings I s'pose—like everything else around your place. Mine never blink an eyelid."

"I don't believe it."

Stas drew himself up with terrible dignity. "Don't contra-bloody-dict me! Calling me a liar now, hey?"

"Why should your hens be all right and mine not? Tell me that!"

"I don't know."

"Of course you don't know!"

"But they are! Come and see for yourself, then, and be damned to you."

Old Oscar spat venomously far ahead as if to mark

the way, and stalked off in front of us without another word. Bruno, Herb, and I unwound our taut stomachs and followed, grateful for the breathing space. We didn't like the job of restraining Dad when, having taken the law into his own hands, he wanted to pronounce judgement and carry out summary execution on the spot. Luckily by the time we'd walked down into the yard they had both cooled off a little. In the twilight the mallee clumps looking down on us were beginning to swell into shadows and blurred outlines.

"There you are, they're just roosting now." Old Oscar pointed vaguely towards the airy dusk, but I saw nothing. "And I only just finished giving them the cyanide treatment a couple of days ago myself."

"Where are they?" Dad asked brusquely. There was not a coop or a shed in sight.

"Everywhere!" Oscar extended his arms like a prophet invoking heavenly blessings. At the same instant a frenzied and clumsy flapping came from one of the mallees—a flapping so thoroughly awkward and ungraceful that, of all creatures on earth, it suggested only one. Dad looked up sharply, squinting in the gloom.

"*There*?" he said.

"There," said Oscar.

"Hellfire! So that's it!" For a rare moment he stood speechless. Old Oscar bridled, sensing another attack, but there was almost as much wonderment and admiration as there was aggression in Dad's voice.

"They roost up in the mallees?"

"Of course."

"You haven't even got a fowl-shed?"

"What I want a shed for?"

"You sprinkle the cyanide around under the trees?"

"Of course."

"Out in the open air? In the breeze?"

"Yes, all around here."

"You never used it in a closed shed?"

"Haven't got one, I tell you."

Dad turned on him suddenly and furiously. "You're an idiot, Aveling. If you ever open your mouth to me about fowls again, I'll fill it up with cyanide and rake it down your throat." And he strode off home, rumbling volcanically and outstripping us at every step.

That was the end of Dad's plan. At one stroke he gave up all hope of ever riding to riches on a hen's back. The cyanide had gone further than killing roosters; it had eaten into his ambition. One by one the remaining ducks and fowls left their heads by the woodheap and their flavour in the soup-pot, until at last we were back to Mum's troupe of old faithfuls again. Now only the empty fowl-house remains as proof of Dad's grand design; that, and the professional way he eyes his six eggs at breakfast every morning.

The Shell

THE green sea swept into the shallows and seethed there like slaking quicklime. It surged over the rocks, tossing up spangles of water like a juggler and catching them deftly again behind. It raced knee-deep through the clefts and crevices, twisted and tortured in a thousand ways, till it swept nuzzling and sucking into the holes at the base of the cliff. The whole reef was a shambles of foam, but it was bright in the sun, bright as a shattered mirror, exuberant and leaping with light.

No wonder the woman on the tiny white beach in the tuck of the cliffs pressed her sunglasses close and puckered the corners of her eyes into creases. Before her, the last wave flung itself forward up the slope of the beach, straining and stretched to the utmost, and then, just failing, slid back slowly like a boy on his stomach slipping backwards down the steep face of a gable roof.

The shell lay in a saucer of rock. It was a green cowrie, clean and new, its pink undersides as delicate as human flesh. All round it the rock dropped away sheer or leaned out in an overhang streaked with dripping strands of slime like wet hair. The waves spumed over it, hissing and curling, but the shell tumbled the water off its back or just rocked gently like a bead in the palm of the hand. Its clean gleam caught the woman's eye as she squinted seawards, and her heart stirred acquisitively. It was something she could wade out for when the tide went back; a way of bringing the sea right into the living room. Just one shell to give artistic balance to her specimen shelf for parties or bridge afternoons with her friends.

Another sea stood up, way out, green and sloping like a railway embankment. It moved forward silently —an immense, mile-long glissade of water coming on inexorably like a sentient thing. The slope steepened, straightened, rose up sheer. And then, almost without warning it suddenly arched, curled over, and pitched down with a thunder that shook the cliffs and set the shallows leaping and seething again. The rocks seemed to shrug and rise, smothered and streaming; and again the outstretched hurl of the last ripples mouthed the sand at her feet.

She drew back the edges of the rug and straightened the gay canvas umbrella. The hamper-case was folded cleverly into a low table, and for the things inside there was shade enough on the rug: thermos and plastic cups, cold meat, and the green and red of lettuce-wrapped tomatoes. Good food and drink, a hot day, and the elemental companionship of the sea. She stood up and waved: "Oohoo! Harold! David!"

The sounds were gripped, bruised, swept away by the sea-tumult, but the two figures high on the cliff caught her movement and waved back. They pulled in their fishing lines and came slowly down the steep path, wicker-baskets dangling and bumping from their shoulders as they walked. Nearer, round the cliff buttress, they emerged more clearly. The man was tall and thin, with a moustache and skin too white for a place like this. But the fish scales on his coat shone like sequins, and he walked proudly. The boy was the son of his father—twelve or thirteen years old and as thin as a stick. But he swaggered with his basket, trying to look like a veteran.

"Any luck?" The woman held up her hand and crooked its fingertips in the man's as he sat down.

"Two nice sweep. Five-pounders, I'd say. And David nearly got a beauty; had him half-way up, but he dropped off."

The boy made excuses. "It's these hooks! They wouldn't hold an earthworm if it kicked!"

His father flung back the wicker lid and the blue gleam of the fish suddenly caught the sun. "Look!"

"Oh, lovely, dear! We'll have one for tea."

"Wait and see what we get this afternoon. They'll be fresher; I'm going down on to the bottom ledge."

"Do be careful, darling."

"I've watched it all the morning. Not a wave within six feet of it. And it's better fishing—you don't lose so many."

He sprawled out lazily and took the cup from her hand. "Lovely spot! I used to come here when I was a lad."

The boy chortled. "However did you get here *then*?" He laughed. A thin, reedy laugh, pale and watery like his eyes.

"The roads haven't changed much. But we walked or rode horses down here in those days, instead of trying to use cars." He smiled at the memory, even while he kept on munching his lunch.

Two gulls launched themselves from the cliffs and swung above them idly, legs thrust back and wings motionless, cupped and cushioned on air. Then they came in to land, running, and stopped two yards short of them, with a benign expression of unconcern. The boy threw a crust. It fell short, but the gull shuffled in towards him sideways, whipped it up at a thrust, and walked back sedately to safety.

The boy scuffed the sand impatiently with his feet, but his mother sighed and leaned back on her arms. "Even the gulls are dignified."

"I can't understand why more people don't come here," the boy said.

"I'm glad they don't."

The man laughed mirthlessly. "They will! Port Lincoln's only twenty miles away."

"Painters and poets should come first," his wife said with sudden feeling; "to see all this before the vandals come, with rifles and bottles."

The man looked out across the leaping foam, puckering his eyes. "There are no seascapes like this east of the Bight. Cape Carnot, Redbanks, Wanna. Giddying cliffs for the climber, and big fish for the liar."

But the boy was kicking moodily at the sand. "I've finished, Mum. Can I go for a walk on the headland."

"David, dear, can't you sit still for a second while we finish our lunch?"

"Can I?"

"There are some very high cliffs along there. They drop sheer into the sea."

"Can I? Please?"

"No, it's too dangerous."

"Arh-h, gosh! Look where we've been fishing all the morning . . . on a little ledge."

"But your father was with you then."

The boy turned to the man, wheedling. "Ah-h, can't I, Dad?"

The man pushed uncomfortably at the sand with the sole of his sandal. "Well . . . just to the top of the headland."

She felt she'd been let down. "Harold!"

"Let him go, Ethel, if it makes him happy. It'll only take five minutes, and we'll be able to watch him all the way."

The boy dashed off around the curve of the beach, his hair brushed up by the wind. The man and the woman lay idle and silent, looking across the bay to the line of cliffs beyond, where the coast curved round from cape to cape, southwards towards Sleaford and Thistle Island and Cape Catastrophe. Everywhere great columns of white spray rose as if in slow motion, like bunches of lace thrust up in fistfuls from below.

"It's never still," she said slowly.

"Looks for all the world like exploding depth-charges. Like some coot rolling them off the cliffs for fun."

She sniffed. "What a comparison! You men!"

"They make nearly as much noise too. Shake the cliffs. Up on the ledge you can feel them vibrating."

"They must bring in some beautiful shells. There's one in that rock just there, see. I'm going to get it later."

"Vanity! Natives races use them for money."

"What if they do. This is a gift to me from the sea."

He smiled weakly. "I read somewhere that we take too much from the sea and give nothing back."

"It always seems to have plenty to spare."

He laughed. "Yes, it can take as well as give. It's old enough to look after itself."

She gazed at the great line of breakers, unsmiling. "One shipwreck would be worth a million shells."

"Perhaps when it feels that the ledger is getting out of balance it just helps itself again."

She folded the cloth, flicking off the crumbs. He

brushed the sand from his arms and stood up. "Well, back to the fish!"

"Don't be too long, dear," she said. "We have to leave by four."

"Whatever for?"

"Mrs Harvery's asked us out to bridge tonight. Remember?"

"What, again?" His voice carried his irritation. "Fancy having to play bridge in a room with walls . . . after *this*." He strode off up the path. The boy, who was on his way back from the headland, ran to catch him up.

Back on the clifftops again, he took up his bait box and lines. Then, guiding the boy, he climbed down very carefully to the lowest shelf. "Easy now, son! Watch your step here." The boy was afraid, but he would never have admitted it to his father. "Gosh, it's steep. You feel as if you're hanging out over the water."

"You are in some places. Don't look down until we reach the ledge."

When they got there the boy was surprised to see how big it was—a wide, flat slab of rock jutting out like a balcony, warm as an ovenplate in the afternoon sun. "It's beaut, Dad!"

"Good spot! I've often fished here."

"Catch much?"

"Lovely sweep. Rock cod, of course. Even snapper sometimes." They sat down with their backs to the cliff and took out their lines. The boy felt as if he was suspended on a platform over a maelstrom, but his father was an old hand at rock fishing and scarcely raised his head. They baited and threw out, far out. The seething foam hissed round their lines with the speed of a shark's rush, and they felt the churn and thud of the water in their hands. They were in touch with turmoil, the shock and fear of it surging up to the boy. But for all that, the tug of a big fish was a stronger pull, firm and evenly sustained. It was on the man's line. He brought it clear of the water, a dark blue sweep dangling perilously above the abyss with the line going straight down into its mouth.

From the beach the woman saw it going up, like a spider devouring its own thread. She waved and shouted, but their senses were numbed by the crash of the surf. The man hauled the fish on to the ledge, twisted it free, and dropped it into the basket. There it flapped for a while under the lid like a spatter of rain on a roof, until it faltered and weakened and slowly died.

He flung his line back into the water in a wide downward arc where a wave caught it and gulped it under again. This time there were no bites. He leaned back against the cliff behind him, loose but quaintly unbending—a young man not yet stiffly old, an old man still vaguely and youthfully supple. The boy fidgeted with his line for a long time, but at last he leaned back too. The shock and thud of the water against the cliff was almost peaceful—a sort of incessant clubbing that numbed and drowsed him by its sheer weight and ceaselessness. He looked up at the cliff edge above him where the tussocky clumps hissed and flickered in the sea-wind, and swivelled his head upwards and around at the noiseless sweep of a kestrel passing over. The man looked up too, gazing beyond the bird into the blue dome of distance beyond. The two of them, man and boy, were peering skywards.

And then, quite suddenly, the sea came and took

them. It stood up and plucked them off the ledge swiftly and decisively, like a hand coming up over a shelf for a rag doll. They barely had time to bring their eyes down to it before it stood six feet high on the ledge, clasped them both, and then fell away, sucking and sobbing as it plunged backwards the way it had come.

Some strange and elemental cohesion, a momentary coalescing of mighty forces, suddenly pitched that great wave up beyond its fellows—twenty, thirty feet up out of a regular sea. A few moments later another, and then a third, towered up and roared high against the rock wall, shooting flares of spray over the topmost edge and drenching the bitter salt-white herbage of the clifftop. Then, as if satisfied with its random muscle-flexing, the sea sank back into its rhythms again like a tigress dozing in the sunshine.

Down in the bay the woman sprang back with a vexed cry as the first big wave seethed in low about her, nosing the sand as if sensing prey. It pummelled her feet, tumbled the gay umbrella in its side, and floated her rug back down the slope of the beach like loot. She ran forward quickly, checked it with her foot, and dragged it to safety, sodden and sand-streaked. Then, on an impulse, she turned and looked up at the ledge on the cliff. It was bare. Water was streaming from it in rivulets, in thick sinewy ropes, in feathery wisps—all falling downwards, downwards, and slowly dying away.

"Harold! David!"

Her scream caught a momentary lull between waves and shrilled out over the little bay. She ran up the steep path in a frenzy, stumbling over rocks and hollows.

"Harold! Harold! David. . . . Oh, David-d-d!"

She reached the clifftop, sobbing and gulping for breath, and rushed forward to stare down on to the ledge. But the last of the huge waves had just come and receded, and the ledge was a slab of clean, dark rock, gleaming like a new tombstone of black marble. It was empty. Only over one corner a single fishing line still ran, bellying out a little and thrumming intermittently in the wind. Two or three glistening drops, shaken clear of it, fell back into the sea like beads.

"Harold! David-d-d! Oh, my God!"

Two gulls, alarmed by her cries, rose effortlessly and hung above her, above the ledge, above the abyss in ironic dumb-show, their legs thrust back and their pink eyes looking down at her, coldly disinterested. Yet perhaps, in their relentless way, they saw more than she.

"They always come in threes, them big fellows," said the old fisherman from Port Lincoln. "And clean out of the blue. You'd have thought Harold would have know that, bein' born here and all."

The police sergeant walked briskly along the cliffs, saying nothing. It was three hours since a woman, hysterical and incoherent, had collapsed on his doorstep with her story.

"Here it is," said the old man. "This'll be the ledge all right." The sergeant looked over cautiously. "No hope of recovering the bodies down there."

"Not a hope in the world. Not even if we knew where they were. Poor devils."

"Horrible way to die."

The sergeant turned to the two uniformed men

with him. "Better search along the little beach—just in case." The constables turned and walked off down the slope, but the old man spat expressively. "Nuh, never find 'em there, Serg. They're down below here —if the sharks haven't got 'em."

Down on the beach the two men searched carefully and fruitlessly. Suddenly one of them stopped and pointed. "Better gather up that picnic gear, Geoff . . . umbrella, rug, hamper, books. . . ."

"Better scout around a bit; it's probably scattered all over the place."

The first man searched down along the shore and stopped near a rock exposed by the ebb. "Look at this shell," he called. "It's a beauty. A green cowrie."

"Never mind about shells. Get the rug."

"I'm taking it home to my wife. These shells are currency in some countries, you know."

"Blood-money! The sea's buying you off!" He watched distastefully as the first man reached down and closed his fingers beneath the smooth pink underside of the shell, as delicate as human flesh. And the sea came gurgling gently round his shoes, like a cat rubbing its back against his legs.

The Fish Scales

THE sea looked as if it wanted you to walk on it. Daybreak was setting the swell with a crust of light, hard and smooth, like milky chalcedony. You wanted to sit down on it and slide over the undulations till your pants were shiny, or toboggan into the troughs just for the fast, free shoot of it.

Tim and I sat on the engine-hatch with our lines out, facing east.

"Like a baker painting the top of a bun," he said.

"Some bun!"

He looked towards the horizon for a bit. It was far off across the rolling plain, fine as onyx.

"Yeah."

"Going to be some fishin' day, too. Perfect!"

"Perfect." Tim pulled in his line and the stone turned to water for a second, herringboned with tiny ripples.

"Daybreak on a cutter out at sea," said Tim. "You've got to see it."

"Yeah, when it's like this."

"Back in Port Lincoln they'll still be snoring holes in their pillows; they probably live half their lives within ten miles of this, and never know."

It was true. Port Lincoln was over the horizon; it was in the next valley. The plain of the sea flowed over the coast, just as the tide of light flowed over the sea. And with it came colour, till the cutter stood up in a pink smooth world, exquisite as the under-belly of a shell.

"Time to go below," said Tim. "Coming?"

"No. I'll fish for a bit."

"I'll whack up the breakfast, then, and see how poor old Bill's getting on; he was crook as a squirting squid last night."

"Right. I'll be down later."

In a way I was glad to be left alone. The truth was that I hadn't been doing too well with the line lately and I wanted to get in a few on the quiet to build up my tally. We were on snapper ground and I knew that if they got on the bite at daybreak I might run up a few.

But I wasn't ready, of course, for what happened: thud! Like a punch to the jaw.

My head flew back and I felt the rick in my neck. The armbone stretched away from the shoulder-blade an inch or two, but luckily my muscles and tendons were pretty elastic; they gave and then took up again. I felt sure I'd hooked a shark or a porpoise or maybe a fifteen-hand sea-horse. Twice he nearly had me over the side when he made a run for it. But I held him. Gradually I worked him up nearer the surface until I could see his outline dimly through the water.

Suffering catfish—the shape of him! He was five feet long! King of all king snapper, with a hump on him like a camel's. In the end I had him right up, just an inch or two below the surface, cruising around as quiet as you like. But it unnerved me just to look at him there—red and coral pink and pearl, gleaming and shining.

But there didn't seem to be any hope of getting him into the boat. I couldn't keep on playing him like this for long, and I didn't want to yell to the others in case I frightened him. Anyway, there was nothing they could have done to help, and I had my pride to think of. I wanted more than anything to surprise them when they came up; you know the sort of nonchalant modesty: "Any luck?"—"Just middling, not a bad snapper over there by the engine-hatch."

Finally I decided to risk everything on the one pull to draw him up over the side and spill him on to the decking. As long as the line held for the first half of the heave when he came up, I might do it, because if it broke then, he'd probably keep coming and fall into the boat anyway. That was usually the way of it. So I braced myself against the winch-head and with a couple of turns wound the line around my waist. Then I took a short firm grip, paused for a deep breath, and *heaved*. My muscles cracked and my eyes bulged.

I didn't know my own strength. In that tremendous pull he came straight up out of the sea like a hunting barracuda until there was only a foot of him left in the water. And in that instant he gave a flick of his great tail like Moby Dick, that hurled him clean out of the sea—that, and the pull I gave.

He shot up over my shoulder in a high curve like a tuna coming aboard, but the impulse of my jerk and his own tail-flip were stronger even than the toss of a tuna pole; he went up, up, over the crosstree of the mast, and then down, leaving the line threaded neatly over the arm.

And so, before I could foresee it, whang, the slack was all taken up and I was lifted off my feet with a jerk as quick as a pistol shot.

There I dangled, exactly balancing the fish, my feet a yard above the deck, treading and kicking the **empty air**. We were the perfect counterpoise; neither of us could pull the other down. And I'm twelve stone.

That'll give you some idea of his weight.

The worst of it was that we didn't hang still. He kept jiggling about, twisting and turning, and I was scrabbling my hardest, too. Naturally, I was trying to weigh my side down; I didn't want him hauling me up towards the crosstrees like a flag at half-mast. So we got to swinging inwards and out, towards one another and away.

One minute I'd be trying ineffectually to embrace his slippery body, and his big wet eye would be staring right into mine; and then we'd swing apart like a couple of contrapendulums, squirming and wheezing before we slapped together again. Then for a change we'd spin round and round in a dizzy whirl, plaiting up the line above us. Face to face and back to back we'd spin, his fins giving me a few short jabs to the ribs, and my elbows getting him a jolt in the gills.

If you've ever been plaited up you know how helplessly frustrated it leaves you; wrapped up like a mummy swaddled in strip bandages. But to be plaited with a twelve-stone fish! It presses your face so hard into his that it's like waltzing with a bear-hugging partner—you can't converse properly because you can't get your head back far enough to see him objectively. At any rate, that's how it went with us until we unplaited ourselves and flew apart again.

Luckily I managed to slow things down after a while by clutching at the mast whenever I shot past, until we finally stopped spinning and just swung backwards and forwards again like a pendulum in an old grandfather clock. Yet that's when the crisis came.

On the second or third swing I could see by the look on his face that he thought he might still have

175

the better of me, and sure enough, the next time we came towards one another he twisted up his powerful tail and fetched me a whack in the stomach, way below the belt, that took the wind out of me with a *wup*. And while I was dangling limp as a gibbet corpse he took his mean advantage, screwed himself right up till he was nearly lying sideways in the air, and gave me a slap on the side of the head that sent my false teeth skidding into the engine-well.

I tell you it's no joke to be slapped in the face by a twelve-stone snapper. It just about did for me. Through the haze I could see half a dozen five-foot fish overlapping and vibrating like a plucked harp-string, and I knew that if he fetched me one more clout like that he'd take me and finish up leaning against the mast himself, playing me on the end of *his* line.

So I made the effort somehow; I had to. Luckily we missed each other altogether the next time, and swung past, hissing hate and looking back vindictively at each other over our shoulders. That gave me a momentary breather and I was half prepared on the next swing. Two can play at that game, I said, and just before we met I brought up my right thigh and kneed him neatly in the belly. A good, shady footballer's groin thrust.

It was his turn to go *wup*! That put some heart and wind back into me, and I was really ready the next time with a long punt kick that caught him in the paunch and sank in with a saggy squelch.

"How's that?" I said.

His eyes goggled glazily and he blew out a lazy string of bubbles. I could see that I was getting the upper hand. A few more swings and he'd be mine.

Then, when he was hanging limp, I'd cut the line, we'd both drop to the deck, and I'd be able to display my catch as if nothing had happened.

The pride before the fall! Especially when you're up a mast with a fish. He had more life in him than I'd bargained for, because on the next swing, just as I was lifting my leg to give him the knock-out, he caught his tail under my feet and flicked me back in a high wide arc like a squeezed pip.

Far out over the wide of the boat I swung, and so did he. Action and reaction! My snapper line was a good one, but it wasn't made for bowing and sawing up in the crosstrees. It had been fraying slowly all the time, and now on the very end of that high outward swing it snapped, and the two of us flew on in a sort of sine-wave.

Same weight, same distance, same speed—we hit the water simultaneously. Down below they would just have heard the one splash.

When I came to the surface to cough, Tim was leaning over the rail, the tears of laughter running off him like bow-spray.

"He's thrown himself in," he yelled down to Bill. "I always said he would."

"I just hooked the biggest snapper alive," I yelled, "but he got away."

Tim was whooping with delight.

"He tied the line round his waist and threw so hard that he tossed himself in."

I climbed aboard, sore and dripping. "He got away," I panted, "a two-hundred-pound snapper; had him aboard, had him right here, but he got away."

Tim looked at the bit of line trailing after me, eyeing the frayed end.

" 'Struth, you must've given yourself a heave, sport," he said, "to bust a line like that."

"I tell you it was a fish that pulled me in," I said, "and by trickery at that. I was joined to him by the middle."

He raised one eyebrow. "Hey!" he yelled. "Come up here quick, Bill, and have a look at poor old Bert's umbilical cord."

And so it was that I lost my fish and my hooks, my sinkers and half my line. . . . Everything in fact, except the shame of my story as they told it. *That* didn't get away.

MORE COLIN THIELE TITLES
from
NEW HOLLAND PUBLISHERS

Storm Boy

The illustrated edition of Colin Thiele's moving story which became a magical film. This is one of the classics of Australian writing for children.

Paintings by renowned artist Robert Ingpen capture the wave-beaten shore and the windswept sandhills of Coorong in South Australia, home of Storm Boy and the pelican Mr Percival.

Storm Boy saves the life of Mr Percival, and in return the pelican helps Storm Boy's father with his fishing and joins in the rescue of a shipwrecked crew. The boy and the pelican prove to be friends to the end.

Magpie Island

The picture book that contains a beautiful story and haunting pictures by Roger Haldane.

Magpie shot off like a bolt from a catapult. He whizzed up into the sky above the hill and then swept down in a fierce circle around the she-oaks, his wings hissing through the air like knives.

Magpie is marooned alone on an island. He is a sad, lonely figure. A castaway. Robinson Crusoe Magpie...

Until young Benny finds him a mate.

Pinquo

Pinquo is a Fairy Penguin, who can swim, skip and dive faster than the blink of an eye.

When Pinquo is wounded, the children Kirsty and Tim take him to Dr Piper, and they all look after Pinquo until he is ready to go to sea.

Later the penguin with the droopy walk and the kinky flipper comes back into their lives, with his new family.

When disaster strikes Sickle Bay, Pinquo leads a mad stampede of a thousand frenzied penguins, to save the townspeople.

Little Pinquo is a hero.

Sun on the Stubble

Bruno Gunther lives on a farm in South Australia, where adventures spring up like wheat shoots.

He has to cope with his stern Dad, his Mother and family—and trickiest of all is the new teacher in town, who is too alert for comfort. Then there are the local arguments, that all seem to flare up around complicated bits of machinery, like water pumps and cars.

All they really need is a little help from Bruno to sort everything out...

This is the first of four books that inspired the television series, *Sun on the Stubble.*

Sun on the Stubble Picture Book

With text especially written by Colin Thiele to accompany *Sun on the Stubble* on television, this delightful book is illustrated in colour with still photographs from the series.

There are lots of fascinating people in the little town of Gonunda—Jack Ryan, who drives his car backwards, Hermann Heinz, 'the big tub of lard', Moses Mibus the storekeeper, Uncle Gus, who gets spooked by ghosts, Miss Knightley, the prim schoolteacher.

Then there is Ebenezer Blitz, the half-mad hermit who wants to blow up the general store.

There are lively girls like Laura Kleinig and Louisa Obst, and the three intrepid Gunther sisters.

And of course there is Bruno. After Bruno's adventures, Gonunda can never be the same.

Sun on the Stubble Omnibus

Bruno Gunther lives on a farm in South Australia with his family: his tough and hardy father, strict and loving mother and three lively sisters.

He gets caught up in a series of incidents, including the feud between Jack Ryan and Mr Heinz, who fight about everything, especially cars.

Not to mention the ghosts that roam the roads at night.

Things really get hot when the whole town goes hunting for the wild dog Elijah, and the great Gonunda fire breaks out.

This is the collection of the four books which inspired the television series, *Sun on the Stubble*. They are: *Sun on the Stubble*, *The Valley Between*, *Uncle Gustav's Ghosts*, *The Shadow on the Hills*.

The Valley Between

Another novel set in Sun on the Stubble country, this is the second book on which the *Sun on the Stubble* television series was based.

Benno Schultz is thirteen and has just left school to work on his father's farm, but he doesn't seem able to keep out of mischief.

He disgraces himself at the beach with his handknitted bathers, accidentally causes his father to break a leg, squirts the Pastor with an enormous stream of milk from Daisy the prize milker, and veers wildly through the night on his old bicycle with a large scarecrow strapped to his back.

Best of all, Benno gets to help Jack Ryan to win the great Gonunda race between Jack's new car and Mr Heinz's horse and trap.

Uncle Gustav's Ghosts

Benny Geister's Uncle Gus meets the first Unseen Presence on a dark, haunted road where murder was once committed.

Ghosts are abroad in this hilarious story set in a South Australian farming community, which helped to inspire the television series, *Sun on the Stubble*.

A spectre, complete with wedding gown and veil, appears after a tin-kettling for two newly-weds, and from then on the fun is fast and furious as a succession of ghosts and ghoulies, phantom horses and poltergeists plague the Geister household and the community at large.

The Shadow on the Hills

Bodo Schneider lives on a farm in the hills near the little town of Gonunda in South Australia.

He loves to range the hills on his own, but one day he gets lost in the mist, and is rescued by the strange hermit, Ebenezer Blitz.

Bodo learns a great deal when he is caught up in Ebenezer's battle with greedy storekeeper Moses Mibus, which culminates in the great Gonunda fire.

Weird old Ebenezer and his faithful but ferocious dog Elijah helped to inspire the final episodes of the television series, *Sun on the Stubble*.

Klontarf

Klontarf is supposed to be haunted. No one ever goes near the old deserted house after sunset, when ghostly figures move through the rooms.

It is the last place Matt and Terry would dream of taking refuge, but when Terry hurts his leg badly, they have no choice.

The terrifying events of that night lead Matt and his sister Jessica into a gripping search for the truth about the eerie old house.

And they discover Klontarf really does have a dark secret.

Fight against Albatross Two

Albatross Two is an offshore oil well. From the moment the giant rig starts drilling off the little fishing village of Ripple Bay, it dominates everyone's life.

For the teenagers Link, Tina, Craypot and Hookie, it is a source of endless fascination.

But then Albatross Two blows out, and an oil spills threatens to kill all the seabirds on the coast. The teenagers get caught up first in an epic battle of man against nature, and then of people against the monster that Albatross Two has become.

It is a battle for survival.

February Dragon

"Go for your life! It's the fire!"
The whole crest of the slope suddenly boiled over with flame, as if a crimson sea had swept the top of the ridge.

The three Pine kids really belong in the bushland. And they have nicknames to match – Resin, Turps and Columbine.

They like fishing for yabbies, taming unusual pets, riding in the local show, and astonishing their teachers.

But their usual adventures are nothing compared to the dire events that take place when somebody lets loose the February Dragon – the dreaded bushfire.

Blue Fin

His father's words were still in his ears: "The boat's in your hands now."

Snook is an ugly duckling of a boy, and he always seems to be in trouble.

His Dad says tuna fishing is a hard life for hard men, and Snook just doesn't measure up.

But the sea takes a hand, with a terrifying whirlwind that turns his whole world upside-down.

Snook's fight for survival in the fishing boat *Blue Fin* is a great sea story that has been made into a feature film by the South Australian Film Corporation.

The Undercover Secret

Times are hard for Jenny Cox's family in the Depression – but she has her beloved river bank and the private world of her friends.

Then her old mate Swampy Marshman dies, and things get frightening. Why is a mysterious stranger searching Swampy's house? Who chases Jenny through the park one night? And what is the meaning of Swampy's strange legacy?

Just when her family are about to be thrown out onto the street, Jenny finds some answers.